GW00499431

Hammer of the North

A Clash of Faith and Steel

Bjorn Wolfe

Shadowplay Communications, LLC

Free Bonus

Download the book "Viking Fervor" free at **Shadowplay.com/Vikings**. Also, get the Audiobook version, also free.

Information on receiving FREE promotional copies of upcoming books and audiobooks

Shadowplay.com/Vikings

Contents

Chapter 1

HOW THE VOW WAS MADE

The hall of the Danish kings in Leira was overflowing with guests on an autumn evening in the year 994. King Harald Gormson had recently fallen in battle, and his son Harald Twyskiegge, also known as Forkbeard, was celebrating his accession feast in the hall of his ancestors. The city was surrounded by a whole host of tents and brush huts. Sixty ships had come from Jomsborg, carrying the noblest members of the famous Viking brotherhood, under their chiefs Haldor Sigvald and Bui the Thick. Visitors and Danes alike were dressed in their finest attire, and the town and camp were alit with joyful festivity. Inside the great hall, ancient weapons and trophies of the hunt were hung on display, the floor was covered with a thick layer of fresh rushes, and the long tables were abundant with food. At one end of the hall, King Harald sat with his chiefs and the Jomsborg nobles, while above them stood the king's throne. Along the hall were placed the Vikings and men of Denmark, with Queen Gunhild and her ladies sitting at the far end. Servants moved quickly through the hall, bearing plates and horns of ale. In the center of the room, between the tables and in front of the king's throne, two skalds played their harps and sang of the great deeds of King Harald and his son, the new king. As the hunger of the guests was sated, they began wondering what vow the new king would make. It was customary for the heirship feast for the new king to make a vow to do some great and noble deed. Seated near Queen Gunhild were two boys who were guests of honor. One of them, fair and ruddy-cheeked, was Sigurd Fairhair. The other, darker with quick, bold eyes, was Vidar Akison, a nephew of Bui and grandson of Palnatoki, the founder of the Viking brotherhood. Though Vidar was only 17, he and his cousin Sigurd were already known for their prowess. Sigurd was particularly elated tonight. Before the feast, King Harald had given him a very fine sword, which he was proud of. Glancing over at him with a smile, Queen Gunhild asked, "Sigurd, have you shown Freyja your new sword?"

Freyja, the niece of Sigurd, sat beside him and her eyes shone with mischievous excitement. "Of course he has! He is going to test it on the giant pine tree by the harbor tomorrow!" she said. This elicited a chorus of laughter from their companions with Vidar teasing Sigurd, "Just make sure you don't bring down the tree and sink our best ships!" Sigurd blushed, but quickly retorted, "Well, at least I never woke the entire camp because I mistook a pig for a spy!" This caused everyone to erupt in laughter, even the Queen joining in the joviality. Suddenly, King Harald stood up and grabbed a magnificent silver bowl. With a calm demeanor, he drank its contents and then handed it over to an attendant. As he walked to the throne, the hall fell silent in anticipation. "As I ascend my father Harald's throne, I hereby vow, with the help of God, to lead my fleet to the land of England. Within three winters, I will drive out King Beornwulf and sit on his throne!" exclaimed the King with unwavering confidence. The hall erupted into a loud cheer, congratulating the King on his grand ambition. Whispering to Sigurd, Freyja commented, "Look how pale the Queen has become. I believe the vow has caught her off guard." Indeed, Queen Gunhild had paled, she knew that such a vow meant war and its outcome was uncertain. Before Sigurd could reply to Freyja, Haldor Sigvald rose from his seat and demanded attention. "Men of Denmark and Jomsborg," he began in his deep voice, "I too shall make a vow, and not a light one at that. As you all know, the heathen Haldor Ragnvald now reigns over Norway, while the rightful king, Tryggvee's son, is either wandering or dead. Thus, I vow to go to Norway and wrest the reins of power from Haldor Ragnvald and restore the rightful king's rule within three winters."

Sigvald took a seat, and the room was silent with amazement until young Vidar Akison shouted out, "Cheers to Haldor Sigvald!" The crowd erupted into cheers as Sigvald's brother, Thorkel the Tall, stood up and swore to follow Haldor. Bui the Thick joined him. Vidar, from the opposite end of the room, joined in with fresh cheers declaring, "I'm with you, and before I return, I shall slay Thorkel Leira for betraying my father to his death!" The excitement continued, with Sigurd eagerly announcing, "I'm with you, Vidar!" The Queen gazed at Vidar and Sigurd with a saddened expression and said, "You are being reckless, my boys. Do you understand the gravity of these oaths? The blood and tears they will cause?" Sigurd respectfully replied, "Noble Gunhild, we understand, but Haldor Ragnvald is a wicked pagan, and so is Thorkel. Besides, I will no longer need to test my new sword on a tree," he said with a sly grin.

The Queen remained silent, observing King Harald. Freyja whispered to Vidar, "That was splendid. I wish I could come along." Vidar chuckled, "You wouldn't last a second. The first war horn would have you down below, trembling." Freyja retorted, "That's not true! I can shoot better than both of you!" Sigurd excitedly challenged her to a match the next day, promising to give her his trained falcon from France if she wins. Freyja eagerly accepted and exclaimed, "I'm going to win that bird tomorrow morning!" She then stood up to follow the Queen out, and Sigurd and Vidar left the hall to head to their tent. As they walked, Vidar asked Sigurd, "What do you think of these vows we've made?" Sigurd thoughtfully replied, "Now that we have cooled down, it looks different. It's one thing for King Harald to conquer England with the resources of his realm, but it's another for Sigvald to conquer Norway with just the brother of Jomsborg behind him."

"But listen, Fairhair, we are Christian folk and Ragnvald is a pagan and a traitor. That will make a difference, certainly! My vow wasn't made in haste. I must avenge my father's death or face shame for eternity." Sigurd nodded, knowing very well that the fierce Vikings would not obey someone who couldn't take revenge for their father's betrayal. As they walked back to their tent, a man ran up, and Vidar recognized him as one of Bui's men in the moonlit night. "Ahoy, Egil, what's the matter?" Vidar asked. "You and Sigurd are summoned to Haldor Sigvald's large tent for an urgent meeting," Egil panted. Without delay, the boys followed him to the big tent where all the leaders of Jomsborg had assembled and took their places beside Bui of Bornholm, who was speaking as they arrived. "It was a reckless vow, Sigvald, but we can't turn back now, and this could earn us great honor, win or lose. Our Vikings are the greatest warriors in the world today and we will give Ragnvald and his son Eirik a fierce battle," Bui proclaimed. A murmur of agreement rippled through the tent, and Sigvald stood up. "Brothers, I was too impetuous in making the vow, but now it's been made, we can't recant. My suggestion is that since we are going to do this, we should do it without any delay. We should call for reinforcements, and go for Norway's capital without delay. What do you think?" Vidar came forward, saying, "I can vouch for my father's ships and men. Let's strike before

Ragnvald has a chance to confront us. We have some of the best men and most of our ships with us. We should leave here by the end of the week, wait at Limafiord for the rest of our men, and then sail towards Hlidskjalf." "Good for you, Vidar!" exclaimed his uncle. "Some say I'm a little plump, but my comrades never complain of my weight in battle!" Everyone laughed, for although Bui was a heavyset man he was one of the most skilled warriors of his time. "I'll offer Sigurd to accompany you if you would like," he continued. The boy's heart danced with excitement, this was precisely what he had wished. Haldor Sigvald smiled. "Is it decided then that we will head for Limafiord from here by the fourth day?"

The response was a resounding "Yes!" The sound of clanging weapons echoed through the council chamber, as the chiefs celebrated their decision with sword and spear striking against their shields. Despite this display of force, the meeting came to a close. Many leaders lingered to discuss finer points and the urgency of sending word to Jomsborg immediately. The young boys returned to their tent, weary from the day's events. As they drifted into slumber, the distant cries of "Skoal! Skoal!" reached their ears, a reminder that the boisterous Vikings and Danes still reveled and made pledges, some of which they would undoubtedly regret come morning.

Chapter 2

THE SHOOTING

E arly the next morning, the three young Vikings were up and about, the smell of campfire still clinging to their clothes. Ready for the day ahead, they grabbed their bows and quivers and set off for town. Their destination was the Kings' Hall, where the brave and fearless Freyja lived with Queen Gunhild. Despite the early hour, the Hall was bustling with activity, as servants scurried about laying fresh rushes and preparing for the day ahead. Sigurd hailed a housecarl, one of the Queen's warriors, and sent him to inquire about Freyja's whereabouts. Five minutes later, Freyja emerged from the Hall, bow and quiver in hand, a bright smile on her face. "Good morning, my Vikings!" she greeted them cheerfully, poking fun at their plans from the day before. "Has your rash resolution cooled off yet?" Vidar grinned in response, his eyes a mixture of amusement and seriousness. "Small chance of that," he replied. Sigurd added jovially, "My falcon is ready to change owners, but I suppose there's no chance of that today." Freyja eyed him playfully. "Oh really? We'll see about that, Lord of Jomsborg and Bornholm!" With laughter and chatter, the group set off towards the harbor, leaving the town behind and crossing through the fields. As they reached the top of the hill overlooking the harbor, they paused to admire the magnificent fleet below them. Sixty Jomsborg ships, along with the vessels of the Danish lords, were docked below. Each ship was adorned with glistening shield rims, while their dragon prows and elaborately crafted sterns were painted with striking designs. Freyja couldn't help but marvel at the impressive display. "Oh, how wonderful it is to be a Viking!" she exclaimed, a hint of wistfulness in her voice. "I wish I were a boy!" Sigurd chuckled. "It's not all it's cracked up to be," he said. "There's the drilling and practice in arms every morning, the weapons to be sharpened. And let's not forget the rowing! My back aches just thinking about those heavy oars." Vidar pointed to a particular longship set apart from the rest, with a gilded prow. "There's our ship," he said. "Sigurd may complain, but he's just as skilled as anyone in the fleet with sword and shield, except for his father and Haldor and you, of course," he added, turning to Freyja. She grinned back at him. "Let's not forget about my falcon. I'm anxious to decide on its fate." The trio left the road and walked for a couple of miles until they reached a desolate stretch of shoreline, rocky and wild. Vidar set up an old wooden shield as a target on a rock a hundred feet away, and the three began to take turns practicing their archery skills.

"Shoot first," commanded Freyja. "I'll go next, then Vidar." Sigurd nodded and selected an arrow. He strung his bow, laid the shaft, and pulled the string to his ear. Twang! The arrow buried itself deep in the shield, just above the center iron boss. "Good enough!" cried Vidar, running forward. But Freyja only smiled and raised her bow. The string twanged, and an echoing answer came as the arrow glanced off, causing the shield to fall backward. "Hurrah!" cried Vidar, picking up the shield. "Full on the iron boss! But you can't do it again!" Sigurd also ran forward, but a sudden cry startled them. They turned to see Freyja struggling with three men, while more were coming from behind the cliff. "Norsemen and spies!" exclaimed Sigurd. Without hesitation, he picked up Freyja's arrow and ran forward, fitting it to his bow. "Your sword!" called Vidar, tearing the peace bands from his weapon as he ran. A shout answered him, and the Norseman ran forward to meet Sigurd. A spear whizzed by his head, and he loosed the bow. The foremost Viking fell with a clash, and as the others paused, Sigurd tore the peace bands from his sword. Next, he was surrounded, struggling and striking, as he realized that more men had appeared from behind the cliff. Now a blade gleamed beside him, and Vidar's voice sounded in his ear. One man was down, two, but others filled their places, and a heavy axe was poised over Sigurd. As it fell, the boy darted in beneath the blow, and his sword fell on the Viking's shoulder. At that moment, something crashed onto his light steel cap, and he knew no more. Sigurd awoke with a dull pain in his head, with his arms tightly bound, and the midday sun beating down on him. As Sigurd raised his head, he saw that he lay on the forecastle of a small ship. Vidar was wounded in the shoulder beside him, unconscious. He saw nothing of Freyja, and a burning thirst consumed him. With great effort, he rose to a sitting position and looked around. They were out at sea and the land lay far behind them. In the stern and waist of the ship were fifteen or twenty Norsemen.

The sound of a voice interrupted Sigurd's thoughts as he twisted around to see a dark man with an unpleasant face standing behind him. The man seemed to be the leader, for he had just come out of a cabin. "That was a stiff crack I gave you, lad, but the steel cap saved your skull," the man said. Sigurd tried to speak, but his tongue was dry, and the man laughed. "Here, Thord," he called. "Bring a horn of water." One of the men in the waist took a horn and filled it from the cask beside the mast, handing it up to the leader who put it to Sigurd's lips. Sigurd drank greedily, and then the other threw a few drops over Vidar, who opened his eyes. He struggled to rise, with a sharp cry. "Thorkel Leira! I-". The effort was too much for him, and he fell back again. Their captor smiled sneeringly. "He is in a bad way to fulfill his vow, eh?" This was the man whom Vidar had sworn to kill, the betrayer of his father! As Sigurd realized this, his head cleared. "Why did you attack us? Who are you?" he asked indignantly. Thorkel laughed again. "Vidar, there, seemed to know my face! You two and the girl, whom I take to be Gunhild's niece, will make a nice gift to Haldor Ragnvald! Great boasts, great boasts!" Sigurd flushed. As he looked at the Viking, his heart gave a sudden leap; framed in the cabin doorway behind, he saw the face of Freyja, her finger on her lips. Making no sign, Sigurd answered the leader calmly. "In that case, leave us alone till we get to Hlidskjalf." As he said this, Sigurd lay down again, turning his back on Thorkel. The latter sneered and stepped to the edge of the forecastle, above the ship's waist. Sigurd opened his eyes and saw Freyja making signs and holding his sword in her hand. Sigurd understood the plan instantly. He silently drew his feet up and gathered his muscles. Thorkel was giving orders a few steps away and paid no heed to him. The boy slowly rose to one knee. He saw Freyja run towards him. At the same instant, he threw himself headfirst at Thorkel, striking him fairly in the waist.

The Viking fell forward with a cry and lay lifeless on the deck. Sigurd was about to follow him over the low rail, but a hand held him back. His arms were bound, but the tight knots were quickly cut, and a sword thrust into his hand. "Hold the ladder," the girl panted. "I'll wake Vidar." Sigurd climbed to the top of the ladder just in time to see the surprised men grabbing their weapons. Arrows whizzed past his head, one after the other, but he parried them confidently with his sword. Freyja ran to the cabin, returning swiftly with a shield. "Here," she said, handing it to Sigurd. The shield protected him from the spear that the first man tried to get him with, but then the man began to climb up the ladder, holding a shield above his head. Sigurd swung his sword with all his might, and it sliced through the shield and the man's body, causing him to fall back among his comrades. Thord, who had brought water to the ship, now rushed up the ladder with an axe. Sigurd was too late to drive his sword, and the axe crashed into his shield, making him fall to his knees. The axe raised again, but Thord fell back with a loud scream, hitting the men below him. Sigurd jumped up, seeing the frightened faces of the men below. He noticed Freyja behind him, bow in hand, and Vidar next to him, looking pale but resolute. "We can't keep this up all day," Sigurd shouted to Vidar. "They'll finish us off with arrows sooner or later." Vidar pointed to the cabin. "We can hold them off in there. Freyja says there's food and water inside." Sigurd laughed. "You look like a Valkyrie, Freyja!

I owe you my life. But what's Thorkel doing?" "Back to the cabin!" Freyja cried in alarm. "They're climbing around the bow to attack us from behind!"

They saw a group of men scaling the side of the ship, making their way towards the bow beneath the dragon's head. With no hope of fending off the entire foredeck, the two boys and Freyja ran for the cabin, locking the door and fortifying it with a sturdy bolt. The tiny room was void of natural light, save for one or two slits positioned high above, just enough to let some air in. "What hope do we have of being rescued?" asked Freyja, collapsing onto a stack of furs. "Not much," muttered Vidar, as Sigurd plopped down beside her. "No one knows where we've gone and we won't be noticed missing until noon, if we're lucky." The Norsemen, realizing that breaking in was as futile as resistance, made no further attempts. The hours dragged on as the three captives came to the grim realization that they would soon be at the mercy of their captors. The vessel was continuing its course northward, propelled by the full force of unfurled sails. It dawned on them that the Norsemen must have spied on the Danes, identifying them as lucrative potential hostages. Vidar, having been roughed up in the process, and the three of them taken captive as soon as they boarded the ship. Freyja, left unguarded, had seized the moment Sigurd regained consciousness and made their way to the cabin. Late in the evening, they heard a familiar voice from beyond the door. "Vidar Akison! Can you hear me?" called Thorkel.

Chapter 3

HALDOR RAGNVALD OF NORWAY

V idar looked at Freyja and then back at Haldor Ragnvald. He knew that they couldn't hold out forever, but surrendering to a traitor was out of the question. "We wish to speak with you, Haldor Ragnvald, before making any decisions," Vidar said firmly. Haldor Ragnvald's eyes narrowed, but he agreed to meet with them later that day. As they waited, the three captives tended to their wounds but refused to bind them up, as it was against the Jomsvikings' strict laws. Pain was just a part of their training, and they endured it without complaint. When Haldor Ragnvald arrived, they could hear his voice outside the ship. Freyja recognized it immediately, and they prepared themselves. Without hesitation, Sigurd opened the door to reveal the imposing figure of Haldor Ragnvald. His beard and hair were as sunny as Sigurd's, but his face was grim and his eyes were shifty. "Will you surrender to me?" Haldor Ragnvald asked calmly. Vidar and Freyja exchanged looks, and Vidar spoke up. "We will surrender, but only if you promise not to bind us." Haldor Ragnvald nodded, and they emerged from the ship, battered and exhausted, but still defiant. As they walked away with their captors, they knew that they had upheld the honor of the Jomsvikings.

Freyja let out a hearty laugh. "So you're fighting against girls now, Haldor? Well, I'll surrender then!" Haldor smiled and affectionately stroked her hair. "Keep the bow, my child. You have done nobly and well. Come to my ship." As they descended the ladder and boarded his ship, Sigurd noticed Ragnvald's graying hair and stiff gait, likely from old wounds. Beside Thorkel's ship, an impressive warship awaited them. As they boarded, the two ships separated. Ragnvald led them to his cabin and spoke kindly. "Sit, and don't be afraid. Thorkel has told me of your tale, especially your vow, Vidar Akison. Your comrades will have a difficult time trying to take Norway from me! By Thor's hammer, they'll need it." He smiled, but it was a reticent grimace. "Freyja," Sigurd interjected, "did Haldor order the attack on us? You know he is my uncle." Ragnvald nodded. "I regret that you were taken, but you will later be returned unharmed, with whatever scat Harald decides is fair. But who are you, Fairhair?" Sigurd grinned. "That is what they call me, Haldor. My name is Sigurd Buisson." Ragnvald whistled in surprise. "Ah, then I have two good hostages! Even better. I'll take you to Hlidskjalf with me, but don't worry, you'll be treated kindly, for now." With that, Ragnvald exited the cabin, leaving the boys to themselves. Throughout the voyage, the boys were treated well and their weapons were returned to them. Under other circumstances, they would have enjoyed themselves immensely. That night, they arrived at the southern end of Norway, and Ragnvald pushed the ship to its limits, eager to reach his kingdom's capital, Hlidskjalf. The next day, they landed at Howes. Ragnvald then sent messengers north over the mountains to his son Haldor Eirik in Raumarike. He also dispatched split war arrows to nearby chiefs as a call to arms. With fresh rowers, the ship hastened to Hlidskjalf. The very fate of Norway was on the line.

That evening, they arrived in Raumsdale to rest and replenish their crew
with new rowers. But they wasted no time and continued their journey at a
fast pace, reaching the city just after the sun had set on the third day. The news
of their arrival had spread like wildfire, and as they made landfall, a clamorous
throng welcomed them with great fanfare. Haldor Ragnvald, the leader of the
group, kept the boys by his side and instructed Freyja to make her way to
the King's Hall, where she would receive the attention and care befitting her
station. He then led the crowd to the imposing temple of Thor, the God of
War, without paying a visit to the King's Hall himself. Haldor Ragnvald, like
the majority of his subjects, held steadfast beliefs in the pagan deities of Norway.
He was the high priest and held the Hlidskjalf temple, the most prominent in
the region, in high regard. As they crossed the threshold of the temple entrance,

Sigurd Fairhair shuddered, and Vidar whispered to him, "Stay strong, Sigurd, stay strong." Sigurd squeezed his friend's hand in response. Being Christians, the boys had resolved not to join in the worship of the heathen gods. The temple was dimly lit by flickering torches. At the sides of the walls, statues of the one-eyed Odin and the enchanting Freya adorned the space. The altar at the end of the room faced the golden sculpture of Thor, and Haldor Ragnvald ascended the steps slowly. As he did so, the gathered Vikings, bonders, and townsfolk prostrated themselves. Sigurd observed the priests bring in a white bull for sacrifice beyond the altar. When he looked around, he noticed that he and Vidar were the only ones standing. Then others saw them and an angry grumble murmured reminiscent of an impending storm. The two boys grew pale at the hostile noise, but they remained firm and upright as Haldor Ragnvald prayed to the God of War. Once he finished, the enraged mutter behind him transformed into a tremendous roar, with people screaming, "Kneel!" "Kneel!" "Death to the Christians!" Ragnvald turned around and raised his hand, silencing the crowd instantly. When he realized the cause of the ruckus, his expression grew somber. "To your knees, to your knees! You dare insult Thor in his own domain?" he barked. "We kneel before none but Jesus Christ," Sigurd proudly voiced his dissent, though his heart was beating rapidly.

Ragnvald's hand shot to his sword, and the crowd advanced, menacing in its fury. But then, as quickly as it had appeared, Ragnvald's hand dropped and he signaled to one of his men. "Harald, take these two to the King's Hall and make sure that no harm comes to them, or your life will be forfeited. Go!" Without a word, the two boys followed Harald through the Norsemen, their heads held high and their hands tightly gripping their swords. The air was thick with muttered threats, but eventually, they emerged into the dark streets, where their guide led them directly to the Hall. Once inside, their door was bolted shut, and at the sound of the lock, Vidar broke the silence. "Whew! That was a close one, old man! I was scared stiff when you answered Ragnvald!" "Me too," Sigurd admitted with a smile. "But we're too valuable as hostages. We didn't need much bravery at all. The question is are we going to stay with Ragnvald?" "Not if we can help it," Vidar laughed. "But we'll have to be cautious. We'll be watched closely, and we'll need to watch out for Freyja." Sigurd nodded in agreement. "True. We'll see her in the morning. For now, she's not in danger." In reality, it was a full week before they saw Freyja again. For six long days, they remained confined to their room with no sign of what the future would bring. Their warder was the same man who had led them from the temple on the first night, and on the sixth morning, he finally came with an unexpected announcement. "You're free to leave the town but don't go too far. Haldor Ragnvald has left, so be watchful. I'm responsible for you." "Where has Ragnvald gone? Is Lady Freyja here?" Vidar asked. "I know nothing about Lady Freyja, but Haldor Ragnvald has gone south to More to return with forces to meet Haldor Eirik." Without waiting for more information, the two boys rushed out of the room and headed towards the great hall. Eventually, they found a woman who directed them to Freyja's room. Upon seeing the boys, Freyja let out a cry of joy. "Oh, I thought you were dead! I saw Haldor Ragnvald once, but he was terribly busy and would tell me nothing. Where have you been?"

Vidar recounted their daring escapade at the temple and their subsequent imprisonment in a few words, leaving Freyja gasping in disbelief. "I would never have dared to face all those men like that!" she exclaimed. "Come over here by the window and speak softly, there are women in the next room." After ensuring the door was securely shut, Sigurd and Vidar joined Freyja at the window. "Last night, I overheard two men conversing in the hallway and I eavesdropped," Freyja began. "Haldor Eirik has amassed a mighty army of men from Raumadale, Halogaland, and Hlidskjalf and is frantically preparing a colossal fleet. Meanwhile, Ragnvald is recruiting men from North and South More. Two nights ago, just before Ragnvald left, a messenger arrived from Eirik carrying their plan. Once Ragnvald has raised as many men as possible, he will journey north to meet Eirik who is making his way south. Combining their forces will yield a force of at least 150 longboats, and they plan to ensnare your fleet in Hildirun Bay." "A trap," Sigurd exclaimed in disbelief. "With that immense force?" "Yes," Freyja confirmed. "However, they fear Jomsborg's warriors, even with the odds in their favor. As such, the peasants will inform Haldor Sigvald that Ragnvald is in Hildirun Bay with only one or two ships, and Sigvald and Bui will hasten there to capture him, unknowingly placing themselves among the entire fleet. Do you perceive their strategy?" Sigurd's eyes blazed. "Ragnvald remains a traitor! This is catastrophic, Vidar. No one can evade such a trap." "I am afraid you are correct, Fairhair," Vidar replied gloomily. "Sigvald will fall into it since he is impetuous and rash, much like your father. There is only one course of action." "What is that?" the others asked in unison. "You, Sigurd, and I need to purloin a boat from the harbor and set sail south. Our chances of reaching Sigvald in time are slim, but we must try. Has Eirik arrived at Hlidskjalf?" Vidar turned to Freyja. "Not yet, but he is expected," she replied. "We might make it!" Sigurd exclaimed excitedly. At that, Freyja stood tall, her voice resolute. "Wait a minute! If you go, I go too. Don't assume you can leave me behind!"

Chapter 4

THE RESCUE IN THE BAY

V idar tried to dissuade Freyja from joining them on the journey. He feared they could get caught in a storm or be captured by Eirik or Ragnvald, but she remained resolute. Freyja would not be deterred from her mission. Sigurd expressed reservations about the journey and the time it would take. Freyja was undeterred; she claimed they needed an additional person, even if it made the trip take longer. Vidar's objections to her going vanished as he laughed at her determination. The three friends made their way to the harbor to find a boat, but Sigurd suddenly had a new plan. There was a ship with yellow eyes painted on its prow. The ship's captain was an old friend of Haldor Sigvald's, and he had been in Jomsborg a month ago. Sigurd suggested they try to convince the captain, Ulf Ringsson, to take them down below Hildirun Bay to meet the fleet instead of taking a small boat. Freyja loved the idea because she feared that their journey on a small boat could end in disaster. Vidar remembered Ulf Ringsson and believed he would be eager to help Haldor Sigvald. Sigurd headed off to find Ulf while Freyja and Vidar made their way back to the hall. As Sigurd wandered around the harbor, he found a boatman and struck up a conversation.

"May I borrow your boat for a couple of hours, my friend?" Sigurd asked, slipping the man a coin. "Of course," the man replied, shoving the boat out and grabbing the oars. "Business hasn't been great lately. I might have to join Haldor Eirik's crew to make ends meet." "Best be careful," Sigurd chuckled. "You never know when you might run into Jomsborg steel." The man laughed and pushed Sigurd off. "No worries, my lord. If I'm not here when you return, just leave the boat on the shore." Sigurd nodded and rowed around to other vessels first, pretending to be curious about their crews before finally reaching Ulf's ship. After slipping under the side facing away from the shore, he scaled over the rail. As soon as Sigurd landed on the deck, a tall figure confronted him. "Who are you, and what do you want?" Sigurd grinned and removed his fur cap. "I'm Sigurd Buisson, hailing from Bornholm. I'm searching for Ulf Ringsson." With a cry of surprise, Ulf took Sigurd's hand and led him to the cabin. "The crew's on land, but it's always better to play it safe. What brings you here? I heard Ragnvald had captured you." Sigurd quickly recapped his adventure and explained the trap set for the Jomsborg fleet, requesting Ulf's assistance. "Of course, Sigurd, of course!" Ulf exclaimed. "I can comfortably stow you, Lady Freyja, and one more person away. But if we're caught, my men aren't capable of fighting." "We'll take our chances," Sigurd replied, immensely grateful for Ulf's aid. "And when can you sail?" "I can't set out sooner than the morning of the third day from now," Ulf answered. "Say, midnight two nights later. My cargo hasn't finished being loaded, and I don't want to raise suspicions. But my vessel, the 'Otter,' is swift. We'll make it down the coast much faster than Eirik and his warships." "We'll be there," Sigurd affirmed. "Will you meet us on land?" "It's better that way," Ulf agreed. "I'll move the 'Otter' further out by nightfall and wait for you with a small boat opposite here."

Sigurd bid farewell with a handshake and slipped over the side of the boat, rowing slowly through the busy waterways on his way back. As he approached a large ship, he noticed some sailors struggling to raise the sail. They appeared to be newly recruited soldiers from the countryside, on their way to join Ragnvald's army, as the ship was a war vessel. Sigurd smiled as he watched them, but his expression turned to concern as he spotted an officer standing beneath the heavy spar the men were hoisting. "He should watch out," Sigurd thought to himself, "if those men lose their grip on the rope, ah, I was right!" As he had feared, the rope slipped from the men, causing the yard to fall and strike the officer, knocking him overboard. Without a second thought, Sigurd shouted and drove his oars into the water, heading towards the spot where the man had gone under. He reached him before the ship's crew could launch a rescue boat. The water was bitterly cold, sending chills through Sigurd's body. However, he opened his eyes and struck downward, seeing the officer's face becoming clearer as he drew closer. But to Sigurd's surprise, the man's face wasn't that of an officer, but that of Thorkel Leira, the traitor! Sigurd paused for a moment, considering leaving the villain to his untimely fate. But he decided that he couldn't let someone die, no matter how much they deserved to. With a quick decision, he gripped Thorkel's hair and began swimming to the surface. Although Sigurd was an excellent swimmer, he was underwater for nearly a minute, and the freezing water made it challenging to keep a hold on Thorkel. Finally, he emerged from the water with a great sigh of relief upon seeing a small boat sailing towards him. After they hauled up Thorkel, Sigurd swam towards his skiff, grateful to be out of the water and back on dry land.

Sigurd realized that being questioned would ruin their plans of escape. Ignoring the shouts of the Norsemen, he hastily donned his fur coat and climbed over the stern of his craft, making his way to the shore. After pulling up the boat, he noticed that his clothes had frozen while he was rowing. Sigurd arrived at the hall without being recognized, and Vidar greeted him with surprise when he threw off his cloak. "What on earth-" Vidar began before Sigurd cut him off with a laugh. "Water, rather, Vidar. Help me get these wet things off first," Sigurd replied. After changing into dry clothes, Sigurd told his cousin about their adventure. Vidar excitedly shouted, "Good for you, old man! I don't think I would have resisted the temptation to let him drown and get rid of the wretch. Did anyone recognize you?" Sigurd shook his head. "I got away quickly and Thorkel was senseless. The yard struck him on the shoulder, so I suppose he wasn't very badly hurt. Don't say anything to Freyja about it." "Why not?" asked Vidar in surprise. "Well," Sigurd hesitated, "she would make a fuss about it, and well, I really wish you wouldn't, old fellow!" Vidar agreed, and they went to Freyja's room to discuss their plans with Ulf. Freyja laughed when they arrived, saying, "You changed pretty quickly, Sigurd." Confused, both boys stared at her. Freyja continued, "Oh, one of my maids just ran in and told me how some yellow-haired stranger rescued our old friend Thorkel down in the harbor and ran off before they could find out who he was. So I knew that it must be Fairhair, here!" "It was me, Freyja!" said Vidar. "If I'd been there, I would have let the scoundrel drown!" Sigurd protested, "No, you wouldn't, Vidar. You might kill him in a fair fight, but you wouldn't let him drown without trying to save him!" Freyja cut the argument short by saying, "Never mind. It was a noble thing to do, Fairhair, and I am proud of you for it." Sigurd blushed and turned the conversation to describe his meeting with Ulf.

"By the way," Vidar interjected, "I discovered something interesting. Our doors are bolted at night, and a man stands guard outside in the hallway. Ragnvald must deem us valuable." Sigurd reflected on the predicament. "The only solution I can think of is coaxing the guard inside, trapping him, then proceeding to Freyja's quarters and seizing her protector before he can raise the alarm. Freyja, be ready on the second night approaching midnight from now, and we will rescue you somehow." "In the meantime," the girl cautioned, "we must not be seen together, or else our intentions may be exposed." Vidar nodded in agreement. "True. We shall not rendezvous again until we come to rescue you, then!" "Very well," Freyja chuckled as they departed. "Goodbye until then!"

Chapter 5

THE ESCAPE FROM HILDSKJALF

That night, under the cover of darkness, the two boys quietly observed the changing of the guards. The hour of their escape was now clear, and they patiently waited for their chance to flee. The following days crawled by with agonizing slowness. The boys kept to themselves, blending in with the crowd, unnoticed. The newfound freedom they longed for was so close, yet so far. As they wandered around town, they stumbled upon the ominous and intimidating temple of Thor. Sigurd couldn't help but shiver in disgust at the barbaric rituals that must have taken place there. He turned to his cousin and wondered aloud when the people of Norway would finally convert to Christianity. He fantasized about one day ridding the land of such heathen temples and replacing them with structures to honor the Christian God. Vidar was skeptical about the likelihood of such a conquest. Norway had fierce and proud leaders, not unlike Haldor Ragnvald, who would vehemently resist any would-be conquerors. He thought it was far-fetched that they would ever become the victors, no matter how noble their intentions. On the second night Harald came to lock them in their room. As he did, he bitterly lamented the loss of his opportunity to join the Jarls. "If it weren't for you two, I could have been with the Jarls by now. It will not be long until your Jomsborgers are finished, " he said. Vidar was alarmed by Harald's prediction, not realizing that Eirik had not yet arrived. However,

Harald quickly dispelled any hope by informing them that Eirik's sixty ships had passed the Firth the day before and would soon join his father at More. However, Sigurd was not one to give up. He recalled Ulf's assurance that the "Otter" was swift enough to overtake Eirik's ships. Additionally, their own fleet may not have advanced this far north yet. So, he ended the conversation with a hopeful mantra, "Never give up!"

"It's true," Vidar agreed. "The men will likely want to land and plunder. But perhaps there's still hope." They stood watch until midnight, relieved when the guard retired. Vidar nudged Sigurd and the latter let out a long, mournful groan. At the third groan, the man outside stirred and undid the bolts. "What's wrong?

Are you sick?" he asked. Sigurd groaned again and muttered unintelligibly, while Vidar threw his cloak over the man's head. Sigurd then sprang at the bound man who struggled furiously until the cloak stifled him. The boys quickly darted off down the hall. Silently, they made their way to the women's quarters without encountering anyone. The man outside Freyja's door was half asleep, so they secured him with little trouble. As the door opened, Freyja emerged donning a dark cloak over her kirtle. "Good!" she whispered upon noticing the bound man. "I'm all ready." They made it to the street undetected, running full speed down the hill to the harbor without seeing another soul. "Otter's" boat waited for them at the water's edge with Ulf, wrapped in a cloak, ready to take them to the ship. As they rowed out to the ship, Vidar recounted their escape to Ulf. Once they reached the "Otter," Ulf leaped onto the deck and quietly commanded, "All ready, men! Slip the cable and out oars." The oars, already muffled, were run out and the men guided the ship through the shipping by the faint light of the stars. A while later, they reached the open Firth, and they hoisted the huge square sail. They were finally on their way home. "Well, that's the last time I'll see Hlidskjalf for a while," Ulf mused as they watched the shores fade into the distance. "It doesn't really matter though. There's little to gain from trading with this country. Next voyage, I think we'll go to England or Flanders. Now, do you want to turn in? I've made the cabin ready for Lady Freyja. You can join the men in their quarters."

By morning, the "Otter" had traveled far down the coast with no fear of pursuit due to the ship's impressive speed. As they sailed south throughout the day, Ulf explained to the boys that they needed to avoid Eirik's fleet, which had passed through the previous day. By nightfall, they turned their prow away from the sea, intending to head toward Hildirun Firth in the morning if the wind held fair. When the boys woke up, they found themselves on a ship chugging along by oars in a dense fog. Ulf reassured them that they were near the coast and that the sun would dissipate the mist soon. However, as they proceeded, the helmsman cried out to Ulf, and the latter rushed to the forecastle to investigate. Ahead of them loomed a sight that befuddled everyone: numerous lights were glimmering through the haze. Unable to figure it out, they gazed for a while until Vidar identified the actual spectacle. It was a fleet, and they needed to change their course immediately. Vidar instructed the helmsman to turn the prow, as they had encountered another powerful armada whose gilded dragon prows glimmered in the sunlight peeking through the clearing fog. Sadly, their efforts to avoid the fleet failed, as the fog cleared revealing the cliffs of Norway and the white sails of a massive fleet just a mile away. The boys' hearts skipped a beat, as they prayed that it was their own fleet. Ulf, Sigurd, and Vidar searched for a sign or symbol that could identify the fleet, and finally, Vidar spotted a sail with a red cross. To their great relief, Ulf recognized it as belonging to Hildirun Firth, the very destination they were aiming for. They swiftly ate breakfast as the "Otter" surged through the waves, and within an hour, Vidar excitedly reported that they'd finally caught up with their own fleet. The boys eagerly scanned the horizon, and sure enough, Ulf pointed to the north where Hildirun Firth lay, and they spotted the fleet heading towards it. They were thrilled to be almost there, and in just half an hour, they would finally be reunited with their companions.

In a matter of moments, they were within sight of the ships. Each one could be distinctly seen, and the group knew Haldor Sigvald's ship at a glance. Ulf veered the vessel in that direction. A marvel of a sight greeted their eyes! Each ship was decorated with vibrant, colorful sails, carefully crafted to resemble beasts and birds. Every vessel was packed with sturdy warriors who brandished their weapons, and in the distance more sails glinted in the sunlight. Vidar spoke up, uneasy. "This is peculiar, Sigurd. I don't see a single ship that belongs to my father. He must have gone on ahead and could be walking straight into Sigvald's trap." Suddenly, a nearby ship signaled them. As soon as they recognized the Jomsvikings Vidar and Sigurd, a colossal cheer went up and spread through the fleet, accompanied by the blare of war horns and clashing swords. The "Otter" drew up to the ship of Haldor Sigvald, and they quickly pulled in the oars. Vidar and Sigurd rushed aboard, with Sigvald expressing his joy at their safe return. They had no time to waste, Sigvald knew by the expression on Vidar's face that something was amiss. The plot of Haldor Ragnvald needed to be shared, and it was not long before a shout of fury echoed across the sea as every man onboard learned of the situation. The news quickly passed from ship to ship, and as the helmsman shouted out the tidings, the other vessels drew near. "We must not delay," declared Sigvald. "Bui has already landed, and his men are pillaging. Ulf, keep Lady Freyja aboard and wait three days at the midpoint of the Herey Isles, a mile or two south. If we have not yet returned by then, go to King Harald at once!" Ulf raised his hand in farewell, and the boys parted from Lady Freyja as the boats went their separate ways. "Let's get you onto your own ship," Sigvald told Vidar as they continued their journey. "Hoist the sails! Row the oars!" He sounded a loud blast on his war horn, and the warriors leaped to their feet. As they passed through the fleet, cheer after cheer emanated in honor of the courageous young lads whose warning had saved them. Blades flashed in the morning light, and with hastened sails, and they quickly set off to warn Bui at Hod Island.

They glided up next to Vidar's vessel, and the two lads leaped aboard. Vidar's seasoned crew gave Sigurd a hearty welcome. These same men had fought alongside his forefathers in countless brutal battles. However, Fairhair couldn't shake the nagging concern for his father, a man he knew had a tendency for reckless behavior. Suddenly, he heard the helmsman howl in terror while frantically waving his arms. "What's happening?" Fairhair bellowed, racing up the ladder with Vidar close behind. Words were unnecessary as they beheld Bui's fleet racing recklessly around the edge of Hod Island, barreling towards Hildirun Bay. The trap had been sprung.

Chapter 6

HILDIRUN BAY

"Forward!" Haldor Sigvald's war horn blared its call. The fleet surged ahead to support their impetuous leader. Sigurd let out a groan of despair, but Vidar reassured him. "Don't worry, Fairhair. Sigvald won't be captured. He'll return when he realizes the trap. However, we're already in it, for Sigvald can't retreat without losing his honor. We must advance and fight like Jomsborg warriors!" Bui's ships vanished around the northern end of Hod Island. Then, as Sigvald organized his fleet into formation, with six ships lashed together side by side, Bui's fleet reemerged with lowered sails and oars churning the water into a froth. Bui's ship was the first to reach Sigvald's fleet. As he stood on the forecastle and shouted his discovery, Sigvald halted him and instructed him to position his ships behind the fleet to form their battle line. Bui rowed past Vidar's ship, and at that moment, Sigurd leaped onto the rail, crying out. There was no time to stop, so Bui's father simply waved as he sped by, exclaiming in excitement, "Skoal, Sigurd! Use your finest weapons today!" That was the last conversation Sigurd ever had with his father, Bui of Bornholm. As the fleet moved forward gradually, one by one, Bui's ships began to lag behind, falling in line behind Sigvald's fleet. The Jomsborg warriors could still have fled, but they refused to do so, as it would defy their laws. The day was now cloudy, and as they rounded the headland into the bay, the wind abruptly shifted direction and blew dead against them. And there, closing in on them, lay the Norse fleet! Radiating out like a mighty crescent, the sparkling oars and steel of Ragnvald's fleet moved forward as Sigvald split his formation into thirds. Due to his father's position and his own prestige, Vidar Akison commanded a third of the ships. Alongside his vessels were Bui's, while the final twenty were commanded by Sigvald. "Look, Vidar!" Sigurd exclaimed as they observed the Norsemen, still half a mile away. "They're breaking up too!" "Yes," Vidar replied bitterly. "But there must be almost two hundred ships over there, filled with warriors. That implies that they'll outnumber each of our groups of twenty out of sixty or seventy!"

Vidar quickly distributed the shirts of steel rings and opened chests of swords and axes for his men. Fully armed, he and Sigurd stood on the high forecastle awaiting the attack. It didn't take long for Haldor Ragnvald's banners to be raised with a horn of war and a rain of arrows and stones to fall upon the Jomsborg ships. Sigvald's banner was also run up, and his men fought back, but the Norsemen had the upper hand with a favorable gale blowing in their direction. Despite this, the Jomsvikings were skilled with weapons and caused great confusion amongst their foes. As the two fleets drew closer, bows were thrown aside, and the spear racks emptied. Sigurd and Vidar stood on the forecastle with their chosen men, ferociously wielding their weapons. Suddenly, with a thundering crash, the fleets collided. "Concentrate on the ship against us!" shouted Sigurd, while a hail of spears was thrown at the large Norse ship grinding into Vidar's. The Norsemen attempted to board, but a hail of weapons pushed them back, and Sigurd cried out, "Hurrah! We will win yet!" Vidar ordered the crew to cast a grapnel at the enemy ship and, with Sigurd and his men, leaped onto the boat. The Norsemen were surprised and withdrew, but a dozen fresh ships appeared on the horizon, and the Jomsvikings knew they had to retreat, calling out, "Back for your lives! Back to our ship!" Surrounded by Norse ships, Sigurd and Vidar could not see the battle on either hand. Nevertheless, they heard a wild shout from Bu'i's ships, and once again, the Norse line shrank backward. As Sigurd turned around, he saw Haldor Ragnvald's ship just behind their own. "Look, Vidar! Order the men to turn their spears on Ragnvald!"

Vidar obeyed the order and a tempest of spears and arrows rained down on their ship. Standing tall on the forecastle, he was almost hidden by the onslaught of weapons. But as the storm of death subsided, he emerged, smiling. His armor lay in tatters and he shrugged it off with ease. A fresh wave of enemies crashed onto Vidar's division, but the higher sides of their ships shielded them from certain death. Although men on both sides were falling fast, the Vikings were not suffering as much as the enemy. The two sides were yet to engage in hand-to-hand combat. But even in the midst of the crowded Norse ships, not a single Jomsborg spear missed its intended target. The Vikings' trained skills had the upper hand against the unskilled levies of Ragnvald. Suddenly, Sigurd laughed hysterically and stumbled. "What is so funny, Fairhair?" Vidar shouted, trying to keep his cool amidst the chaos. "Nothing," replied Sigurd. "Just an arrow in my arm. Nothing more. Nothing to worry about." And he continued fighting, drawing the arrow through the wound and snapping off the barb. But soon after, another arrow flew past his head and buried itself in the ship's rail. A third arrow followed, grazing his helmet. Sigurd realized he was being targeted. Looking across the fleet, he spotted the face of Thorkel Leira on one of the ships below, preparing to take another shot. Using his shield, he intercepted the next arrow and flung a spear in retaliation. The weapon struck Thorkel's shield with tremendous force, piercing it and causing Thorkel to stagger. But before Sigurd could follow up, a fresh attack drew his attention away. When he looked back for Thorkel, the ship had retreated. Suddenly, a bolt of lightning tore through the darkening sky accompanied by a rising wind. And seemingly out of nowhere, Haldor Ragnvald's ship burst into flames, with Haldor himself standing tall in the stern, brandishing a hammer like that of Thor. A roar of terror erupted from the Jomsvikings as they mistook the figure for that of the war god himself. The lightning was followed by a shower of hailstones as large as eggs that exploded on impact, pelting the Jomsborg men mercilessly.

The Norse host was invigorated as they shouted, "Thor with us, the gods fight for us!" Their war horns pealed even louder as they pressed forward, certain that Thor and Odin were on their side. However, Vidar's cry of anger and dismay echoed through the chaos, "Sigurd! Look yonder!" To their astonishment, Haldor Sigvald cut the lashings of his ships and fled, leaving the Jomsborg men in terror. Their morale was shattered because they believed that Ragnvald was right and that the gods were truly fighting for their enemy. As Sigvald's ship cut through the press, Vidar took a spear from the deck in a fit of rage. With a curse, he hurled it at Haldor but missed, striking the helmsman at his side. The fleeing ship disappeared from sight in a flash, and soon after, ship after ship followed Sigvald in his flight. Despite being left hopeless, Bui remained true to his vows, fighting on steadfastly as his Norse attackers retreated for breathing-space. As Bui's ships pursued, they made a fatal error by cutting their lashings, just as fresh Norse ships drove down on them. Breaking their solid front, they were soon surrounded, and boarders began to pour in. Watching helplessly, Sigurd saw Bui's men slowly clear the deck before his father was surrounded by the Norsemen. He fought on steadily, locked in single combat with a gigantic Norseman, wielding an axe. Suddenly, Bui slipped, and the axe whirled above him, striking his helmet and wounding him terribly. However, Bui recovered quickly, cutting down his foe before leaping to the rail. "Overboard, all Bui's men!" his voice rang out loud and clear. Just then, the fight closed in on Vidar once more, and Sigurd caught a glimpse of his father in the midst of a battle with a giant Norseman. Although he fought valiantly, Bui eventually fell beneath the waves, dying as a Viking should.

The Jomsborg fleet was in pieces, each ship fighting fiercely until the very end. Each vessel was boarded and emptied of its men, and finally, Vidar's ship was the last one left. As the Norse enemies poured over the sides, the Vikings finally unsheathed their swords and axes, with the young boys in front. Again and again, the wave of foes surged across the bulwarks, but the Jomsborg warriors held their ground and pushed back against them. At last, a deafening cry sounded from behind, and those who were still alive retreated slowly to the forecastle, fighting with all their might. Then a strikingly handsome man of great stature, leading his soldiers, appeared on the prow and made his way towards Vidar. The two men met in a violent clash of swords, and the tall man, clearly a respected leader, fell beneath Vidar's strikes. But he was not finished yet, springing to his feet even as his men swiftly surrounded Vidar. Sigurd let out a fierce yell and rushed to his friend's side, but it was too late. The savage crowd surged towards him but recoiled before the Jomsborg warriors' axes. Vidar lay motionless, and Sigurd, standing over him, faced the noble-looking leader, brandishing his axe. The enemy's sword flashed, and for a moment Sigurd struggled to fend off the storm of strikes. Then his axe landed on the leader's helmet, and the man staggered back. But before Sigurd could press his advantage, he slipped on a pool of blood, saw a sword coming towards him, let out a battle cry, and fell across Vidar's body. With Vidar and Sigurd gone, the battle was over. Thirty-five ships had fled with Sigvald, while twenty-five had stayed with Bui and Vidar. One by one, Haldor Ragnvald's men boarded and cleared the ships, showing no mercy. Some of the Vikings were killed by sword and spear; while others chose to follow Bui's example and sank beneath the waves. In the distance, the white sails of Sigvald shone for a moment, then disappeared to the south.

Chapter 7

HOW VIDAR KEPT HIS VOW

"That's all of them, I reckon twenty in total. Wait, this one's still wakin' up. Give him a hand, will you?" Sigurd's eyes slowly opened to the sight of two men leaning over him: his handsome adversary, and Thorkel Leira. The young boy struggled to stand up with the former's help. It was mid-afternoon and the storm had passed. The Norse fleet surrounded the Jomsborg ships, and deck after deck was littered with the fallen. In the midst of it all, Sigurd caught sight of a small group of Jomsvikings with their arms bound, then the memory of Vidar hit him. Thorkel held a horn of water to Vidar's lips, and as Sigurd knelt beside his friend, he was wondering why his sworn enemy would help them. It wasn't long before he found out the truth. Vidar looked up, spotted Thorkel, and flung the horn away as he tried to get up using Sigurd's arm. Before he could speak, they were both seized and their arms were bound, after which they were led to the waist of the ship to join the other captives. The men erupted in praise. "A great fight, it was, eh Vidar?" muttered Biorn of Bretscade (also known as Wales), an old Viking who had served under Vidar's father and grandfather for over twenty years. "I've seen many battles, but none like this." "It's a sad day for the brotherhood, Biorn," Vidar replied weakly, "when even Haldor himself turns tail and flees." There was an angry murmur among the group before Sigurd asked, "Who's that tall fella, and what's gonna happen to us?" Biorn nodded towards some boats nearby. "We're being taken ashore, but I don't have any idea why. I don't know that person either." A group of Norsemen then surrounded them, binding their wounds and exchanging rough jokes about the fight. They examined the Jomsvikings with awe and wonder: a name so famous, who had fought so valiantly against overwhelming odds. Soon, the tall man and Thorkel arrived on the shore, and Vidar exclaimed, "I've figured it out, Sigurd! That handsome devil must be Haldor Eirik, son of Ragnvald!" At that moment, the handsome man walked up to the captives.

"Jomsvikings," he addressed them, "you fought fiercely and with great courage. My heart is heavy that Haldor Ragnvald has ordered no mercy be shown. If it were up to me, I would spare your lives." Vidar, with a brave smile, responded, "It is the luck of war. If we had won, I doubt Sigvald would have spared Ragnvald. But Christians have more merciful ways than those who follow Thor and Odin." The other Norseman blushed, turning to Thorkel. "I do not wish to kill these helpless men," he protested. Thorkel, with his cruel smile, retorted, "It is my great pleasure to put an end to Vidar Akison." Vidar cried out, his voice ringing with challenge, "You were too scared to face me in battle, Thorkel! Will you release my bonds and fight me now with sword or axe?" The Norsemen around them murmured their agreement, but Thorkel shook his head as he toyed with his weapon. As Thorkel went to speak with the handsome chief, old Biorn leaned into Sigurd, whispering excitedly, "Now is your chance, Fairhair, take it!" Sigurd nodded as Thorkel returned. "Start with the leaders, Thorkel," he goaded with a racing heart, praying Biorn's plan would work. Thorkel stepped forward and stood in front of Sigurd. "Since you want to die so badly, let it be." "Wait!" Sigurd yelled as Thorkel lifted his axe overhead. "Someone must hold my hair so it isn't defiled." One Norseman stepped up in admiration of Sigurd's bravery and gathered his long, fair hair in his hands. Thorkel's axe swung, but as it descended, Sigurd jerked his body with such force that the axe plunged into the earth, and Thorkel tumbled forward. The Vikings all roared in laughter as the chief stepped in to hold Thorkel back. "What is your name, brave boy?" the handsome man asked. "I am Sigurd, son of Bui," replied Sigurd, looking into the chief's eyes with admiration. "The Jomsvikings are not all dead yet!" "You are indeed a son of Bui," the chief exclaimed. "Will you take life and peace from me?" Sigurd replied with challenge, "If you have the power to give it!"

The man stood tall and announced, "He offers who has the power to give: Haldor Eirik Hakonson." "Thanks, Haldor," breathed Sigurd, visibly relieved. "I will accept it." Old Biorn's whisper had proven correct. Thorkel scowled and angrily grasped his axe. "Though you spare all these men, Eirik, Vidar shall not escape me!" he bellowed. With a swift motion, the axe spun towards Vidar. But, just in time, Biorn threw himself against Thorkel's legs. The man stumbled, and the axe fell at Vidar's feet. Without hesitation, Vidar seized it and fulfilled his vow. An uproarious cheer filled the air! Norsemen loved nothing more than courage in battle. They gathered around Vidar, gazing in admiration while Haldor Eirik smiled and said, "Will you also take life, Vidar?" "That I will," replied Vidar, "if you will also spare my men." "Free them from the ropes," commanded Haldor, and it was done. As the sun began to set, the Norsemen hastily assembled a camp near the shore, with Haldor Ragnvald encamping across the bay. The men sat around their fires and spoke softly, as Sigurd and Vidar were called to Haldor Eirik's fire. Eirik greeted them warmly, saying, "Sit down and eat, friends, for I have much to consider. My father commanded that no Jomsviking should be spared, but I cannot fathom why I spared you two. Perhaps it was because you were merely boys, full of courage. Where do you intend to go now?" Vidar glanced at Sigurd, who nodded in approval. He then recounted the tale of Ulf and Freyja, who awaited their return just a few miles away. After Vidar finished speaking, Haldor sat in thought for a moment. "I believe my best course of action is this," he said. "If I send you both off together, my father will send a ship after you to end your lives. I will not let my promise be broken. I will travel by land to the mountains, to my own earldom. Vidar, come with me, I can protect you. Sigurd will rejoin Ulf with the eighteen remaining Jomsvikings. Within a month at most, I will send you home, Vidar." "An excellent plan," exclaimed Vidar. "Don't you agree, Fairhair?" Sigurd nodded, knowing he would miss his cousin. Still, there was no other option, and thus it was decided.

The morning after bidding farewell to Vidar, the Jomsborg men and Sigurd launched three small boats. Eirik had armed them well and gave them many presents. Vidar stood on the shore, waving farewell as they pushed off. "I'll see you at Jomsborg next month," called Sigurd. "Farewell!" With a fair wind, the three boats quickly sailed down the bay, rounded the end of Hod Island, and arrived at the Herey Islands in just an hour. Sailing between the largest and smallest islands, they reached the bay where the Otter was anchored. A shout of greeting was heard as they approached. Ulf Ringsson jumped onto the rail and asked, "Who won the battle?" Sigurd pointed to his wounded men and replied, "These are all that are left of the Jomsvikings." A cry of horror followed as Ulf staggered back. "Impossible! Where is your father Bui, Haldor Sigvald, Vidar Akison, Aslak Holmskalle? They cannot be dead!" "Some are even worse off," said Sigurd, climbing the rail wearily. "Vidar is safe, my father is dead along with Aslak. Sigvald and his men have fled home again." While Freyja greeted Sigurd, and his wounded and weary men came aboard, Ulf remained stunned with amazement. "Fled! Fled!" he muttered. "The Haldor himself false to his vows!" He could not believe it, for it was the most sacred law of Jomsborg that no Viking should turn his back on a foe. Sigurd told of the fight, while the excited sailors questioned his men. As he finished, Freyja sprang forward. "You're wounded, Sigurd! See, your arm is all red, and your head is bloody!" "Yes, bind it up," laughed Sigurd bitterly, "for the Jomsborg rules are shattered with the brotherhood forever!" Then he reeled and would have fallen save for the strong hand of Ulf. They carried him to the cabin, and while the men set sail, Ulf, who was skilled as a leech, extracted the broken arrowhead and bound up the wound. The other wound on his head was not dangerous and Sigurd soon fell into a deep sleep, not waking until the afternoon. The rocking of the ship told him that they were out at sea, so he hurried to the deck. To his surprise, the land was out of sight, and a heavy gale was blowing. "So you're awake!" cried Freyja. "How do you feel?"

Sigurd let out a hearty laugh, relishing the idea of another battle. But his joy quickly dissipated when he remembered his father. He felt a pang of sadness, but Freyja seemed to sense his turmoil and wisely turned the conversation towards other matters. "We had barely set sail when this ferocious gale descended upon us," she said, motioning towards the tumultuous sea. "Ulf thinks it's only going to get worse." Sigurd surveyed their surroundings and noticed the sail was tightly furled, with everything else securely battened down. The only exception were the three little boats they had used to reach the "Otter," now safely tied up in the stern. "Ulf, my friend!" he called out in greeting, glad to see a familiar face. The captain gripped his hand warmly, a look of solidarity passing between them. "If my father Haldor were here, he would say that Ran, the ocean queen, was trying to finish what Thor and Odin had started at Hildirun Bay," Sigurd remarked, turning to Freyja with a playful smile. But the captain's had a grave look on his face. "Make no mistake, Sigurd. We are in for a rough ride. Thank the gods the Otter is sturdy, because we are far off course to Denmark. It's quite possible that we'll be blown off even further." The wind howled and the waves rose higher, threatening to swallow them whole. Sigurd knew that their journey was far from over and that a perilous future awaited them on the horizon.

Chapter 8

SKOAL, TO KING THORSTEIN!

S igurd and Freyja relished the sharp wind and saltwater splashes as they stood at the bow of the ship, the "Otter". However, the churning seas grew to mammoth proportions, and they were soon forced to seek shelter in the cabin. Except for those on watch, the rest of the crew stayed below deck. Sigurd trusted in the vessel's sturdiness and the capable command of Ulf to see them through the tempest. "How strange it all seems," Freyja mused later. "Just weeks ago, we had all gathered for my uncle's heir-ship feast. Now, the Jomsborg order is crumbling, Vidar is far away in Norway, and we're being tossed about at sea. I wonder what happened to your falcon?" Sigurd grinned. "Who can say? But don't worry, we'll soon be back with Queen Gunhild. Hey, Ulf, what's the news?" Ulf arrived, soaked from head to toe, and gave a grim report. "Not too good, Sigurd. This is the fiercest storm I've ever seen. I shouldn't have sailed this time of year. But we must trust in God and weather through it." For five endless days, the "Otter" careened before the raging gale, everyone onboard preoccupied with the exhausting labor of bailing the ship, which was repeatedly drenched by towering waves. If not for the 18 Jomsvikings who traveled with Sigurd, it's doubtful they would have made it this far. They all worked mechanically, their every moment consumed by the fierce elements until they were physically shattered. On the fifth evening, Sigurd was conversing with Freyja in the cabin

when a deafening crash and screams startled them. Rushing outside, they saw
that the mast was gone, its jagged remains jutting into the sky. Ulf shouted, "The
mast! Sigurd, I've done what I could! If the mast had held, we'd have been alright,
for the storm is dying. But an hour ago, I saw land in the west. We can't sail away
from it now."

Freyja turned to Ulf, a look of despair etched on her face. "Do we even know
where we are?" she asked. Ulf shook his head, uncertain. "It could be Scotland,
the Orkneys, the Fareys, or even Vinland. We're lost, and it's in the hands of
God now." Despite their uncertainty, they persevered, managing to rig enough
canvas to the damaged mast to keep the "Otter" on course throughout the night.

As the morning broke, a long line of cliffs loomed ahead. On the forecastle, Freyja grabbed Sigurd's arm urgently. "Why don't we escape in those boats?" she yelled over the howling wind, pointing towards the small boats lashed in the stern. Sigurd and Ulf had not even considered this option, the Viking ships usually being small enough to be drawn ashore without the need for a boat. "You're right, Freyja!" Sigurd exclaimed, rushing to Ulf. But Ulf shrugged off the suggestion. "What's the point? We'll only prolong the inevitable. The moment we hit those cliffs, it's all over." However, Sigurd was not dissuaded. They readied the boats, loading them with provisions and weapons to ensure their survival. "We need to leave before the ship strikes," Ulf shouted. "Otherwise, the waves will take us all down." Sigurd nodded and led Freyja down to the gathering crowd around the boats. With the cliffs now in sight, Ulf motioned for everyone to board. Sigurd took charge of one boat, with Ulf and Biorn of Bretscade commanding the other two. With a sharp command, Ulf ordered them to launch the boats into the water, and they were soon paddling frantically, the waves threatening to overturn the vessels. Despite the treacherous conditions, the small boats persevered, finally docking safely on the nearby shore. As they dragged themselves onto land, they were relieved to find they had arrived on the coast of Greenland.

"Goodbye, old Otter!" Ulf called out as he was the last to leave, and just as they were pulling away, they witnessed the ship lurching and reeling wildly. "We barely made it in time!" Sigurd said to Freyja, who was in his boat. "She hit the rocks but luckily scraped over this time. Next time, however-." As he spoke, the ship leaned over to one side, sending a flurry of foam into the air. But they couldn't dwell on it, as they were now focused on battling the rough waters. Sigurd steered while the men rowed, and the waves carried them toward the cliffs. Suddenly, Ulf raised his hand and waved it, indicating where they should head. Sigurd followed closely behind Ulf's boat, and as they approached the shore, he saw a small stretch of beach before them. With one final push, the men guided the boats onto the sand and jumped out to drag them up onto dry land. Sigurd helped Freyja out and looked around. The cliffs didn't seem as steep now, and he realized they could climb them. Ulf joined him soon after, and the captain was feeling more optimistic. "Lady, your plan saved us!" Ulf exclaimed to Freyja. "I had given up hope. Strange that I never thought of using small boats myself, but we rarely use them. Now, Fairhair, what should we do?" Sigurd gazed out at the wreckage of the Otter being pummeled by the waves. "I suggest we unload the arms and food from the boats, climb the cliffs, and see where we are. We have over twenty well-armed men, and I doubt anyone will dare to attack us." Ulf nodded and gave the necessary orders. The group, led by Sigurd, Biorn, and the other men, made for the cliffs. As Sigurd anticipated, they didn't present much of a challenge for the Norsemen, who were used to climbing the fjords back home. In just thirty minutes, they stood atop the cliff, surveying their surroundings.

The landscape before them was filled with thick woods, rolling hills, and valleys, but no sign of any human settlement. The storm had subsided, and the sun began to break through the looming clouds. In the distance, they spied a glistening river. A cry of delight rose from the men as Ulf pointed to the river and suggested they head there for fresh water and a meal before deciding on their next move. They left the sea and entered a forest. The autumn season had stripped the trees of their leaves, but the forest was alive with fresh and green pines. Biorn, perplexed by the new land, voiced his thoughts, "I don't think it's Scotland, Fareys, Orkneys, or Wales. It could be Ireland, but I've never been there." Freyja interjected, "Isn't Ireland where men say Thorstein Tryggveson is king?" Sigurd replied, "Indeed, but it's vast, and we can't be sure of finding any Northmen there." Ulf countered, "Well, let's forge ahead boldly. If we are in Ireland, we're lucky as they say it hosts the finest civilization in Europe." "There used to be," old Biorn interrupted with a growl, "just like in Wales, my homeland, but the pagan Vikings have nearly ruined it all." Their journey led them to the banks of a broad and sluggish river. They rushed down to the shore, drinking greedily and washing the salt from their skin. Sigurd poured Freyja a horn of fresh water, but they didn't have long to enjoy it, suddenly when Biorn's cry pierced the peaceful moment. "Back! Back! Draw your swords, men!" A rain of arrows fell upon them, felling two sailors, and a wild roar came from the trees. The Jomsvikings sprang into action, climbing up the bank and forming a defense line around their leaders while the others took their positions.

Amidst the dense trees, dark figures flitted about. Sigurd commanded, "Form a shield wall, men! Keep your spears at the ready." The Vikings' bows were useless, their strings having been thoroughly soaked. Powerless against the onslaught of the arrows, they waited with no defense until Sigurd bravely shielded Freyja, protecting her from harm. Suddenly, a horde of men clad in woolen tunics, some even wearing armor, wielding spears and axes, rushed out of the forest with a menacing war cry. The attackers charged, and Sigurd gave the signal. The attackers crumbled as the heavy Jomsborg spears ripped through them, sending half a dozen to the ground. But just as they were dealing with the onslaught, a war horn echoed in the background. A voice bellowed in Norse, "For the Cross! Charge, men!" A group of steel-clad men swept through the woods, forcing the others to flee in a mad dash. As the group disappeared into the forest, a man approached the stranded Vikings. Even though Sigurd stood tall, he was surprised to see this man tower head and shoulders above him. He was broad and frank with blue piercing eyes and red hair that flowed over his golden armor. He draped himself in a blue cloak, wearing a gold helm and a gold-linked byrnie. His shield bore a massive red cross. The man locked eyes with Sigurd and asked, "Are you, Christian men?" "Yes, we are," replied Sigurd, delighted. "Where are we? Who are you, the one who rescued us so opportunistically?" "You're on the coast of Ireland, a mere three miles from my city of Dublin. The Irish wouldn't have dared to come so close if they hadn't thought I was cruising somewhere else. I am Thorstein, son of King Tryggve of Norway." The Jomsvikings gazed in wonder at the handsome chief. Old Biorn blasted his war horn, and the Vikings cheered, "Skoal to King Thorstein! Skoal!"

Chapter 9

HOW FREYJA FARED FORTH

"Thanks, friends!" smiled Thorstein, and Sigurd was in awe of the handsome and regal man standing before him. "Who are you, young sir? And who are these men? Truly, I have seldom seen such a fine group of warriors, wounded as they may be!" "I am Sigurd Buisson of Bornholm, King, and with me is Freyja of Vendland, niece of Gunhild of Denmark. This is Ulf Ringsson, captain of our ship, and as for my men, they are the last of the Jomsvikings." "What!" Thorstein exclaimed in amazement, throwing down his weapons. "Tell me your tale, quickly! I heard of Harald's accession feast, but nothing of what followed. Has Sigvald won Norway?" Sigurd recounted the battle at Hildirun Bay, and Thorstein's face grew dark. As they continued on their journey to Dublin, Thorstein told them of his own adventures. He had fled to Russia after his father's murder, became a wandering Viking, and was later baptized. He had then come to Ireland and won the kingdom of Dublin, ruling alongside his brother-in-law, Thorstein Kvaran. "We spotted your ship from the castle," he explained. "So I came out to aid any who might escape. Now, what do you intend to do?" "As for that," replied Sigurd, "I don't care much, but Lady Freyja here must be returned home." "Then will you be my man?" inquired Thorstein. "That I will!" Sigurd exclaimed, turning to his men. "Listen, Jomsvikings! What say you to taking service with King Thorstein?" "Aye!" the men roared, clashing their arms, and Thorstein smiled. "That pleases me well, Sigurd, for a few Jomsborg men are worth a hundred others. As for Freyja, she must take her chances. It is too late in the season for ships now, and I fear she must remain with us until spring. However, that can wait. There is the city." As they crested a hill, Dublin came into view and the Jomsvikings marveled at its beauty: a town with towering walls and strong fortifications unlike any they had seen before. They rode through the streets and were quartered in the palace, where Thorstein assigned rooms for Ulf, Sigurd, and Freyja.

Fresh new garments were sent to all, and they joyfully reconvened at the great hall for the midday meal. There, Thorstein introduced his visitors to Queen

Gyda, his brother-in-law, and other important members of his court. They quickly became engrossed in conversation, forgetting their previous hardships. After the meal, Sigurd led his Jomsborg men into the hall and knelt before Thorstein's high seat. He vowed to obey and serve the king, with the others following suit. Thorstein then bestowed each man with a shield adorned with a large red cross. However, Sigurd received a stunning golden helmet boasting a dragon in the same precious metal, with outstretched wings. "I won this helm in Russia," Thorstein grinned, "so may the dragon always face my enemies!" Sigurd was thrilled with the gift worthy of a king, and expressed his gratitude to Thorstein. The following day, he was appointed to serve in the court-men or bodyguard, and began his new duties. A week later, the first snowfall arrived, yet Freyja was not dismayed since she had given up hope of returning home before the spring. Thorstein's court was a pleasant place, and both she and Sigurd thoroughly enjoyed themselves. Queen Gyda grew fond of Freyja, who had a cheerful demeanor and a joyous heart. Sigurd's wound soon healed, and by Yuletide, both had adapted to their new environment. Sigurd became quite attached to King Thorstein, who was high-tempered yet just. In warlike exercises, no one could match him. He would often stroll down to the harbor, have his men row out a warship, and then walk along the oars as a challenge. To top it off, he would sometimes juggle knives or balls, never losing his balance. Thorstein was very interested in Sigurd, whose nickname "Fairhair" had followed him from Jomsborg. The king contributed to Sigurd's repertoire of sword tricks learned in school. As Yuletide came to a close, a ship sailed into the bay, a rare sight since ships usually did not voyage during winter. The visitors aboard were traders from Norway, causing the court to be filled with astonishment.

One evening, as Ulf sat eating his meal, he suddenly leaped to his feet. "Who was that man that just walked past the door?" he exclaimed. The King shot a swift, keen look at the captain before replying, "That is Thorir Klakke, who arrived today from Norway with his brother Thorkel, bearing news and goods for trading." Ulf warned, "Then beware of him, Thorstein, for I have often seen him in deep conversation with Haldor Ragnvald. He is here for no good,

I think." Shortly after, Thorir and Thorkel entered. Both were short, dark, and well-dressed, but their eyes constantly roved beneath their low brows. Thorkel's face, in particular, was powerful yet sullen. Thorir started slightly at the sight of Sigurd, but Thorstein greeted him kindly, and he sat down silently, falling into low conversation with his brother. For several days, nothing occurred except for Thorir's frequent audiences with Thorstein. But at every meal, Sigurd noted Thorkel's gaze fixed on himself or Freyja although it dropped before that of Sigurd. This puzzled him, for he could not see why Thorkel should be interested, and it also angered him, for he saw plainly that Freyja did not like it. A week or two after the arrival of the Norsemen, Thorstein and Sigurd were talking together while Freyja and the Queen were busy with their sewing. Suddenly the King exclaimed, "Sigurd, how would you like to visit Norway next summer?" The boy started, meeting the King's eye eagerly. "Nothing better, my lord!" Thorstein smiled. "Well, Thorir urges me to take the realm of Norway from Ragnvald, as is my right. He says that the bonders are not satisfied with Haldor's rule and that it would be an easy task to overthrow him. What think you?" "Well," responded Sigurd, "if Haldor Ragnvald could overthrow the might of Jomsborg, I think it would go hard with others who attempt his kingdom." Freyja, who had been listening earnestly, broke in: "Perhaps, King Thorstein, Ragnvald might have sent this man to bring you into his power!" Thorstein stared at Freyja for a moment, then his blue eyes lit up with a fierce light, and his fist came down on the table. "As I am a Christian man, that is it! Beware, Thorir Klakke! If I go to Norway, it will not be as your master expects!"

"The manly Ragnvald controls a strong force of sixteen Jarls," said the Queen, her eyes glinting with speculation. "But not all of them will remain loyal for long. If each Jarl governs one of the kingdom's districts, perhaps you may find an opening that way, Thorstein." The King nodded, his expression resolute. "Regardless, I will need a formidable force. Once I rule Norway, I swear upon my sword that I will uproot paganism from the land and bring it under the Cross of the White Christ! The Hammer of Thor will disappear from this land!" For a moment, the King's handsome face hardened with determination.

Then, as he rose to bid Sigurd goodnight, his expression softened again. A few days later, Sigurd felt Thorkel's gaze becoming increasingly intolerable. The boy decided to warn the man to stop staring at Freyja so insolently. As he passed through the narrow, dimly-lit streets on his watch, three men leaped out from a doorway, catching him off-guard. Despite being outnumbered, Sigurd stood his ground, drawing his sword and using a nearby wall to shield himself. The men attacked him one by one, their blows shattering his lightweight shield. But Sigurd's men were nearby, and he called out their battle cry. The attackers redoubled their efforts. One of them struck Sigurd's shield with enough force to shatter it, but Sigurd's sword landed a fatal blow on the second man's shoulder. The third man's sword, however, dealt a grievous wound to Sigurd, causing him to stumble and fall over the body of the man he'd killed. At that moment, torches lit up the lane, and a loud shout caused the assassins to flee. The attackers shouted in anger as they saw Sigurd lying in the street, but they had already fled. Biorn, one of Sigurd's men, picked him up off the ground. Thanks to the gift of Thorstein, Sigurd emerged from the skirmish unscathed. Nevertheless, there was a noticeable dent in his helmet from the force of the blow. Biorn rifled through the possessions of the slain man, and his companions let out a cry of recognition. "He is one of Thorir Klakke's crew! To the King!"

"Stop!" called out Sigurd, his voice echoing through the night. "Let us wait till dawn. They won't be able to escape and the King won't appreciate being awakened from his slumber." Although it was a reluctant decision, the Vikings agreed and Sigurd took his post once more. However, the night was far from over. Two hours past midnight, a guard from the harbor raced up to Sigurd, sounding the alarm. "Sigurd, Thorir Klakke's ship is leaving and they aren't responding to our signals. Hurry!" Sigurd called to Biorn and together they raced down to the harbor. The ship, a trading vessel, could be seen slowly making its way to the harbor's entrance. Without hesitation, Sigurd hopped into a light skiff moored by the edge of ice. A dozen men rowed with all their might to catch up to the fleeing ship. "Easy now, men," Sigurd commanded as they closed in on the vessel. "Why are you leaving Dublin? Return and make your case!" But the ship only replied with a mocking voice. "What business is it of yours, young rooster? Go back to Jomsborg and-" "Help, Sigurd! Help!" A cry interrupted, but silence quickly followed. Something splashed into the water beside Sigurd's boat and Biorn retrieved it. "That was Freyja's voice! Get closer!" Despite their efforts, only a mocking laugh answered as the ship hoisted its square sail and vanished into the night. "It's no use," Biorn sighed. "We should turn back. Look, I found this." Biorn held out a piece of wood with something scratched onto it. Sigurd and Freyja were the only ones who knew the secret of Runic writing, known exclusively among the priests and high-ranking chieftains of the Northmen. As they approached the landing, Sigurd was filled with a terrible dread. "Quickly now, we must hurry!" he shouted, urging his men on. As they drew ashore, Sigurd held the piece of wood up to a torch to get a better look. The inscription was too faint to read in the dim light.

Chapter 10

FAREWELL TO DUBLIN

Biorn and his band of Vikings huddled around, their faces etched with confusion as Biorn struggled to make sense of the markings. None of them could read Runic, it being more of a shorthand than anything else. A cry of dismay rang out from Sigurd. "Listen, men!" he bellowed. "Thorkel bears me to England! Rescue, Sigurd! Come, men, to the palace!" The Vikings echoed his words, their Jomsborg battle-yell piercing the slumbering town and reaching up to the castle. "Bring Thorir Klakke, but harm him not," commanded Sigurd. "While I arouse the king." But Thorstein, the king, was already awake. He had been roused by the loud clamoring outside. Sword in hand, he made his way to the great hall just as Sigurd charged in at the other end. "What's going on?!" bellowed Thorstein, his eyes wild with anger. "Justice and vengeance, King!" panted Sigurd, handing Thorstein the piece of wood. Thorstein took it and, by the light of the torches, read the message. "What does it mean?" he asked. "Freyja of Vendland has been kidnapped, Thorstein, and I was attacked by three men in the streets. I killed one of them, and he was a man of Thorir Klakke's-stay, here is Thorir now." Biorn and two Vikings stormed in, dragging a trembling Thorir. Thorstein quickly grasped the situation and confronted him. "What does this night's work mean? Where's your brother?" he demanded. Thorir stammered, "I don't know, my lord. Is he not in his rooms?" Then, with a hint of boldness creeping in, he added, "Am I accountable for Thorkel's doings, Thorstein? What do you mean?" Thorstein locked eyes with the man and Thorir squirmed under his scrutinizing gaze but did not back down. "Go to your rooms," Thorstein spat, dismissing him with contempt. He then turned to Sigurd. "Now tell me the full story." Sigurd recounted the attack and the ship's escape, as well as Freyja's cry. "I sent men to her rooms," he finished. "Here they come now." As if on cue, the men entered, followed by Queen Gyda and some of her ladies. Gyda had learned of the tumult from the Vikings and explained how a messenger had lured Freyja out of her chambers an hour before, claiming that Sigurd was gravely injured in a fight. "Come with me, quickly," Thorstein ordered Sigurd, and they made their way to the castle ramparts. The sun was just starting to rise, and all they could see on the horizon was a small, white speck out at sea.

"The proof against Thorir may not exist yet, so we shall deal with him later," declared the King. "But that man over there has brought shame upon me, and he shall be executed. Fairhair, select men from my court and gather the fastest longship in the harbor, the 'Crane.' Thorkel has already commandeered his brother's ship, so you will soon catch up to him. The 'Crane' is already supplied with everything you need, so hurry and depart within the hour." "Thank you, Thorstein," replied Sigurd. "I was just about to ask you for this favor. I will bring along my own men and thirty of yours. Thank you for your kindness and most of all for your friendship, Thorstein." The King smiled sorrowfully. "I have few acquaintances, Sigurd, and you, though new, are most loyal. Go with safety and don't forget about me, for it's still storm season." Just as Sigurd walked away, the King stopped him by a sudden impulse. "Wait! Give me your hands." Sigurd, bewildered, held out his hands for Thorstein to take. "Now, swear to me again, Haldor Sigurd!" Overwhelmed by this unforeseen honor, Sigurd tripped over his oath and welled up with tears. "I don't need an oath to promise allegiance, King Thorstein! When you have seized Norway, being friends with you is all I desire." Tears came to Thorstein's eyes as well. He unbuckled his sword-belt, throwing it over Sigurd's shoulders. "I may not have any earls yet, but here is my Haldor-gift, my friend. Goodbye!" Sigurd shook the King's hand and hurriedly left, commanding his men and selecting thirty of Thorstein's men. He sent them down to the "Crane" with Biorn and followed them shortly after bidding Ulf farewell. The captain would have joined Sigurd, but Thorstein had ordered him to convey a message to an Irish king further inland. As Thorstein had said, the "Crane" was fully equipped for their journey, and they set sail with the wind. As they left the harbor, Sigurd informed his men about his promotion and it brought about a cheer from his followers. The Jomsvikings were proud to have such a gallant leader.

Even though the title carried no land, every chief of noble birth aspired to become a Haldor or Earl, for the Jarls were second only to the King. With the wind light, the oars were run out, and the "Crane" sailed southward under full speed. Thorkel's ship was out of sight, but Sigurd knew his destination and was confident of overtaking the other ship before nightfall. "Old Biorn, why do you think Thorkel is heading for England instead of Norway?" Sigurd asked. The elder paused for a moment before answering, "Well, Haldor Sigurd, I believe Thorkel is a cunning man. If he took Freyja to Norway, he would gain nothing, but by taking her to England, he can profit much. King Beornwulf would pay a high price for a hostage from King Harald of Denmark." "I see! Then she will not be harmed?" Sigurd enquired. "Of course not, Haldor. At least, not until she reaches England, which may never come to pass. Beornwulf is as treacherous as Ragnvald himself, and if Freyja falls into his hands, it would be bad business for her." They did not catch up with Thorkel's ship as soon as Sigurd expected. Only in the mid-afternoon did the helmsman shout while Sigurd ran to the forecastle and saw a small white speck far ahead. "Lower the sail and get out all the oars," Sigurd ordered. "We cannot catch up with them today, so it's best to let Thorkel think he is safe." The "Crane" sailed under her oars until nightfall when the sail was hoisted, and the oars were taken down. The wind freshened toward midnight when Sigurd handed the watch over to Biorn. At dawn, Biorn woke Sigurd up. "Come, Haldor! A squall from the west has hit us, and it's daybreak," Biorn said. Sigurd followed him to the deck and saw the reefed sail and "Crane" running before a squall of wind and driving snow. There was nothing to do, but wait until sunrise. As the full day broke with heavy snow flurries, a shout went up! Not half a mile away, Thorkel's ship also ran before the wind. "Men, shake out the reefs! We may as well take our chances and ensure we get her," Sigurd commanded.

Biorn halted Sigurd and pointed to a dreary gray line on the horizon. "England, or Wales rather, Haldor! It would be fruitless to take Thorkel's vessel in these turbulent waters. Our ships would shatter like kindling-wood." Sigurd begrudgingly conceded and trailed Thorkel's ship as the Welsh coast grew more prominent in the distance. The sky cleared, yet the sea remained rough, precluding any attempts to board. "I recognize this place, Haldor," the helmsman hollered. "Remember that great headland, Biorn?" "Aye!" Biorn replied. "Observe how the coast slopes there, Sigurd? That's Wales, where my kinsfolk reside. We are entering a vast inlet that stretches deep within the land. And to the right is the Saxon kingdom of Wessex. Six years ago, we voyaged there and pillaged a town they call Bristol. It seems that Thorkel intends to make a landing along the Saxon shores." Sigurd was transfixed by the towering cliffs until Thorkel veered his vessel to the east. Sigurd noted that they were, in fact, within a massive inlet. The "Crane" stayed within a distance of the fleeing ship but did not draw any closer. "Where do you suppose they'll transport Lady Freyja if they succeed in landing?" Sigurd wondered aloud. "To King Beornwulf's castle in London, no doubt," Biorn replied. "Although there's no hope of them escaping our pursuit." "Prepare yourselves, men!" Sigurd commanded soon after. "The seas are settling, and we will engage them now." Thorkel, too, observed the shift in tide and made a swift turn toward the shore, rowing with great haste. The two ships, only a few hundred meters apart, skirted along the low-lying shoreline. But then, Biorn let out a howl of fury: "He'll slip away yet!" Thorkel's ship, just beyond the craggy headland, had turned in toward the coast. The "Crane" altered their course, dropped their sail, and with all oars at full throttle, rushed forward. Before them, they saw Thorkel's vessel and his crew sprinting out. Meanwhile, an armed band from the town above raced to meet Thorkel.

Sigurd didn't waste any time waiting to see what would happen next. Instead, he leaped overboard from the "Crane" as it scraped against the sand and ice. Biorn followed suit and waded ashore with him. While they were among Thorkel's party, Sigurd spotted the flutter of a dress and knew that there was little point in searching the other ship. So he dashed up the hill with haste. Suddenly, a barrage of arrows rained down upon Sigurd and his men. The cry of "Death to the sea-wolves!" echoed through the air. Sigurd, Biorn, and one other man were far ahead of their group, sprinting as fast as they could. But as the trap was sprung, a group of Saxons appeared out of nowhere and surrounded them.

Chapter 11

AT BEORNWULF'S COURT

Sigurd sheathed his sword with a decisive flick of his wrist. The Saxon hoard hesitated, unsure of what to do next. One of their bravest stepped-forward. "You'll find little plunder here, Vikings; only hard knocks. You had best put to sea again," he taunted. "We are no Vikings or sea-wolves," retorted Sigurd. "I am Haldor Sigurd Buisson, one of King Thorstein's warriors from Dublin. And, I am in hot pursuit of these men who fled up to the town. Two days ago, they abducted a noble lady from Thorstein's very own castle, and I seek to rescue her." The Saxon leader gasped in astonishment while Sigurd's company soon caught up with him. The Saxons raised their bows in a menacing manner, but the leader gestured for them to stand down. "You look rather young to be a Haldor," the leader mused out loud. "But, if your story is true, then we have indeed done wrong. The leader of the other party said he was pursued by sea-robbers and was on his way to King Beornwulf. So, although he was Northman, I gave him safe conduct. What proof have you for your tale?" Sigurd's heart sank at this unexpected development. But, he knew he had to win the Saxon over if he wanted any chance at retrieving the abducted woman. "Does my ship look like a Viking dragon?" Sigurd stated confidently. "If we were Vikings, we wouldn't be abroad at this time of year. Look, I wear the Cross, and my men are from Thorstein's courtmen. You can see that from their shields and weapons. We are all Christians and no followers of Thor." The Saxon leader came forward and shook Sigurd's hand heartily. "I beg your pardon, Haldor. I am the warden of the coast, and I must do my utmost to defend it from sea-rovers. My name is Haldor Edmund, and now I recall that there was a woman or rather, a girl among the other party." "She's a noble lady from Denmark," Sigurd clarified, not wanting to reveal anything about the woman's true identity. "Now, can't we follow these men to the town?" Haldor Edmund paused to consider the request. "Of course, but they told us they were on the King's business. I sent a man with them to procure horses at once. I'm truly regretful about this whole mess, Haldor." "You did your duty," Sigurd reassured him. "There's nothing to be done now." He looked over to Biorn. "What's your counsel, old friend?"

"We must catch Thorkel," said Biorn. "I suggest you follow him with the Jomsborg men. I will take the others and the ship, and we will proceed to London by sea." Sigurd nodded in agreement but turned to Edmund, the Saxon, for confirmation. "Can we buy horses in the neighboring town?" Edmund assured him that they could, and Sigurd quickly selected his trusted Jomsborg men before rushing to the town. They rode hard, but Thorkel had a head start and had taken the best horses, leaving the Jomsborg men with exhausted mounts. As they passed through Malmesbury and Wantage, Sigurd and his men were surprised by the size and civilization of the cities. Wessex and Sussex had gone untouched by the Danes, creating a society far richer and more advanced than anything in the North. Sigurd marveled at the land's beauty and remarked to his men, "If these Saxons had kings like ours, King Harald would have a hard time indeed before taking the throne of England." When they arrived in Reading, they discovered that Thorkel was only half a day ahead. They pushed on to London with relentless speed, reaching their destination by evening. The next morning, Sigurd arrived at the palace and announced himself to the chamberlain, causing a stir in the great hall. Sigurd had grown into a formidable figure in the past few months, now larger than his age, with golden hair that flowed over his shoulders. He wore a blue cloth kirtle and waist and was armed with the magnificent sword given to him by Thorstein, with a hilt wound in gold and ivory carvings on the scabbard.

The chamberlain led Sigurd to the high-seat where King Beornwulf sat. Sigurd knelt briefly before rising again. The king had a deceitful countenance that made Sigurd nervous. His heart sank when he noticed the mocking face of Thorkel among the courtiers. Once the chamberlain announced Sigurd's name and title, the King stood up. "Greetings, Haldor Sigurd! The men of King Thorstein are always welcome at court. We look forward to Thorstein's return. You seem quite young to hold such a high title under such a great man!" Sigurd responded appropriately before making his request. "My lord King, I ask for your aid. Amongst your men, I see Thorkel Gormson, a Norseman who recently abducted a lady from King Thorstein's castle. I have followed him closely, and since he is here, Lady Freyja can't be far away." King Beornwulf looked taken aback. "What is this? Thorkel is a peaceful trader, and he just arrived here yesterday. He said nothing about a lady!" Sigurd stood his ground. "Regardless, she is with him, and King Thorstein sent me to rescue her. I must ask for your help, King Beornwulf." The king called Thorkel to stand before him, which he did with a sly smile on his face. Beornwulf asked him about Sigurd's allegations. "Nothing, my lord. I don't have any woman with me, and I recently arrived on the west coast where I was trading." Beornwulf looked at Sigurd, and Sigurd knew that he was being made fun of. The king likely held Freyja as a hostage. "You must have been mistaken about Thorkel, Haldor Sigurd. He is a kind-hearted man," said the king, his voice full of false kindness. "I can aid you if needed. You and your men can stay in the palace." With Thorkel's mocking smirk and these words, Sigurd lost his temper. He stepped forward and shouted, "There is no mistake, King Beornwulf, and you know it well!"

Do not think that you will avoid Thorstein's wrath with fancy talk when he hears of this. As for you, Thorkel," Sigurd's eyes flared as he turned on the man, causing him to cower in fear, "Watch yourself! If I catch you outside the palace, I'll kill you like the mutt that you are!" "You've crossed the line, Haldor Sigurd," the king retorted sternly. "I promised to help you with this matter, so bring your men to the palace immediately, and we'll search for the lady." Sigurd returned to his men with a heavy heart. He knew that the king's command meant he and his crew would be closely monitored, with no way to rescue Freyja. When he delivered the unpleasant news to the men, they were just as outraged as he was. But, there was nothing they could do, and they took up residence in the palace that afternoon. Thorkel made sure to steer clear of Sigurd. The Jomsvikings roamed the city streets freely, marveling at the shops, while Sigurd instructed them to keep an eye out for Freyja. The days passed, and Beornwulf tried to placate his guests with a pretended search of the city and kind words, but Sigurd eventually decided to take matters into his own hands. By mid-February, he was eager to return to King Thorstein. After dinner, he huddled his men together and declared, "If we're to locate Lady Freyja, we must do it ourselves. I suspect she's being held in the palace's women's wing, so mingle in those quarters and act as if you're shopping. I'll do the same, and with any luck, Lady Freyja might either spot us, or we'll pick up some clues." Sigurd was treated with great fanfare, but whenever he stepped out, he sensed that someone was watching him. The next day, he visited the shops near the women's quarters of the palace. One of his men approached him as he strolled, saying in a hushed tone, "Come with me, Haldor." Sigurd followed, chattering, and the man led him to the third window from the edge.

Sigurd's heart leaped with joy as he spotted a scrap of blue and gold cloth hanging from the corner of the window. It was unmistakably from Freyja's scarf, and he knew they had found her. As he looked up, a face appeared but quickly vanished as he gave a sign of warning. "We have found her, sure enough! And now to rescue her," he exclaimed upon returning to his room. Later that evening, a wild shout erupted from the next room where Sigurd's men were gathered, and Biorn strode into Sigurd's room, his face partially covered with bandages. "What is this? Wounded, Biorn?" Sigurd asked, concerned. "We met a Danish ship four days ago, Haldor, and she stopped to talk with us," Biorn explained. "Up to your old tricks, sea wolf! What did you talk about?" Sigurd laughed. "The price of swords, mainly. The Danes finally decided that ours were better, so we gave them Thorkel's old trading ship and brought the Dane with us. She's brand new and as fast as the 'Crane'. It was hard work, though, for I had only thirty men, and they were double that. We lost ten killed, and half of us are wounded, but that is no matter. Now for your story." Sigurd quickly filled Biorn in on the situation with Freyja. After a moment of silence, Biorn spoke up. "It is no light matter, Sigurd, to brave Beornwulf, but I think we had best carry off Lady Freyja. Once aboard the 'Crane', we would be safe. But how to do the business?" "By craft only, Biorn. Freyja saw me today and knows we are here. How to get a message to her?" "That is easy enough. You write it, and I will shoot an arrow into her window tonight," Biorn suggested. "Good! I never thought of that," Sigurd replied, grateful for the idea. He quickly got some parchment and wrote the message. "I told her that tomorrow night we will wait beneath her window. She must contrive to let herself down, and if necessary, we will fight our way down to the 'Crane'. Is she below the bridge or above it?" Sigurd asked. "Below. I will go down tomorrow and bid the men be ready to receive us. We must get some fresh water on board too," Biorn said, already planning their next move.

An hour ticked away before Biorn turned up once again, breaking the silence. "The arrow flew obediently true, Haldor. I lingered a while and witnessed a light flit across her window three times," he reported, sounding victorious. Sigurd affirmed this with a grave nod. "Excellent. She comprehends our message. Let us prepare the 'Crane' for tomorrow then, and make certain we are back before dusk. Have a couple of boats at the water-stairs near the end of this alleyway." "Rest assured, Haldor," Biorn replied before quickly making his way back to the vessel.

Chapter 12

THE FLIGHT FROM LONDON

The return of Biorn and the discovery of Freyja's whereabouts occurred in such close proximity that Sigurd saw an opportunity to seize. Twice a day, Sigurd was seated close to the high-seat at meals and engaged in friendly conversation with King Beornwulf, but Sigurd could sense an underlying tension. He knew that the King would eventually make a move to get rid of him, a Northman that brought trouble to his reign. At the noon meal, the day after Biorn's arrival, King Beornwulf called Sigurd to his side and asked about the progress of the search. Sigurd took on a somber demeanor and replied that he had no news, hoping to buy time. The King appeared relieved at Sigurd's response, and Sigurd couldn't help but suspect that the King's spies had discovered his recent visit to the shops. Thorkel, who Sigurd had not seen in days, was undoubtedly keeping a close eye on him. That evening, Biorn arrived at Sigurd's room with a rope and grapnel, and Sigurd asked if the "Crane" was in shape. Biorn confirmed that all was ready, and two large boats were waiting at the stairs. Sigurd voiced his concerns about being followed by Thorkel, but they decided to wait for the streets to empty before making their escape. An hour later, Sigurd roused his men, and they set out, splitting up into two groups. Sigurd and three others headed to the corner of the palace where Freyja's window was located. The palace was surrounded by a high wall with a small garden inside, and Freyja's rooms were on the upper floor of the two-story building.

As they approached the towering wall, Biorn hoisted the grapnel up and flung it with all his might. It held onto the wall. Sigurd grasped the rope and scrambled up, hand over hand. Once at the top, he switched the rope to the inside and slid down, crouching beneath the window. The veil of darkness shrouded everything above him, but Sigurd wasted no time. He threw a stone at the shutter, it swung open and something tumbled out. He caught the object, which turned out to be a makeshift rope made of torn curtains. He held onto it firmly, allowing Freyja to slide down to his side. Silently, Sigurd welcomed her with a firm handclasp before bringing her to the wall. They climbed up together, and within minutes, they were standing in the street. Old Biorn greeted Freyja warmly and draped a dark cloak over her dress. They immediately set off for the river. When they met the dozen men who remained with Sigurd, he dispatched them ahead with Biorn to prepare the boats. Freyja and Sigurd followed after them. Within ten minutes, they were going down the stairs, pushing off the boats. Freyja and Sigurd stood on the prow of the leading boat. "Hurrah! You're finally free, Freyja!" Sigurd cheered under his breath. Freyja, however, yanked him back suddenly as a spear whizzed by him. A yell ensued, and a dark mass materialized in front of them, revealing a sizable boat brimming with men. Sigurd decided to abandon any pretense of subtlety. "Row, men, row!" he roared. One of his men fell to the ground after being hit with a spear, and before he knew it, the other boat had collided with theirs. Standing on the prow, Sigurd unsheathed his sword and took a swipe at the man in front. Meanwhile, Biorn tried to shield their boat from the other craft. Then he heard Thorkel's scornful chuckle ringing in his ears. As Sigurd attacked his foe's shield, Thorkel's boat hook ensnared Sigurd's byrnie and almost dragged him overboard. "You possess some sturdy armor, my friend Sigurd," Thorkel jeered as the young man staggered. Sigurd struggled to free himself from the hook, but before long, he realized he wouldn't be able to. "Take Freyja aboard and set sail, Biorn!" he shouted. But instead of resisting the boat hook, Sigurd jumped towards the prow of Thorkel's boat. As he did, Biorn yanked away with a cry of shock from Freyja, and Sigurd found himself alone, surrounded by his enemies.

As the boy sprang aboard, Thorkel was pushed back and he staggered. Sigurd swiftly drew his sword and with a single blow, cut him down, freeing himself from the hook attached to Thorkel's steel shirt. As he looked around, he noticed the second boat had arrived, forgotten in the heat of the moment. Sigurd struck down another man and bounced back among his followers, instructing them to follow Biorn to the "Crane". Without hesitation, the men set off and quickly caught up with the first boat, with no sign of pursuit. Now safe, Sigurd breathed a sigh of relief. Biorn asked if all was well, and Sigurd assured him that Thorkel would not be bothering them, at least for some time. As they left, Sigurd heard some shouting from behind them and saw torches darting to and fro, but they were beyond capture. Soon they passed below London Bridge and were soon aboard the Crane. The men welcomed them with a hearty cheer and rejoicing. Sigurd took Freyja to the cabin while Biorn took over the ship, oars at the ready. Once settled, Sigurd asked her to share her story. Freyja recounted that Thorkel came to her room around midnight with a note in Runic claiming that Sigurd had been injured and was asking for her to come. She noted that it was strange for Thorkel to visit but went anyway. As soon as they left the palace, Thorkel's men seized her, brought her to the ship, and locked her up in a cabin. Fortunately, Freyja managed to scratch on a piece of wood, threw it out the window, and called for Sigurd. Thorkel threw a cloak over her head, and she was treated well enough after that. When they landed, Thorkel made Freyja promise not to escape if he left her free. Once they arrived in London, King Beornwulf treated her beautifully. He gave her many gifts and assigned women to attend to her. Sigurd was furious at the villainous Thorkel and told Freyja everything the king had said.

"I was kept locked inside my room," Freyja said. "But truly, I had no reason to complain. Then one day, I caught a glimpse of you across the way in the marketplace, and you know the rest. I made a rope from the curtains and here I am now." Sigurd chuckled. "Shall we remain here in the cabin, or venture out to the deck?" "Out to the deck, by all means. But why do your crew refer to you as Haldor?" Sigurd recounted his recent conversation with Thorstein, and upon hearing it, Freyja averted her gaze. "I suppose after this, you will hold me inferior to you that-" "Nonsense," Sigurd intervened, laughing. "Enough of this foolishness, let us go topside!" Freyja cheerily darted up to the deck, and Sigurd followed. They raced down the Thames, which rarely froze over during winter, and any trace of pursuit faded away. Since it was too dark to make out anything in the starlight, Freyja went to bed, Sigurd surrendering the cabin to her as he took charge of the ship. Biorn relieved him after a short while. When dawn broke, they were a great distance from land, and their boat was well stocked with furs, keeping everyone warm. Suddenly, Sigurd looked back and exclaimed, "Look over there, Biorn! What vessel is that?" The old Viking gave a wicked cackle, causing Sigurd to recall the ship that Biorn took while on his way to London. "She only had fifteen men aboard, Haldor, for there was no more room on the 'Crane' to spare. But yesterday, I found twenty Scandinavian men in London willing to work for Thorstein; they are with us onboard now. She may come in handy." Sigurd nodded in agreement. "Indeed, she is exquisite. Where did you find these men, Biorn?" "Oh," Biorn replied offhandedly, "they were prisoners of Beornwulf's, so I offered them a chance to sail. They weren't being closely watched, so here they are!" Sigurd cried out in alarm, "What have you done? Don't you realize that this could bring down the entire Saxon army on us?" Biorn shrugged his shoulders. "There were only a pair of Beornwulf's longships on the water, Haldor, and as they were left unguarded, some of the men rowed over last night and almost destroyed their masts." Sigurd grasped Biorn's hand tightly. "I'm sorry Biorn. I should have known you better. That explains why we weren't followed. Now what is our next step?"

It was sheer madness to be venturing out to sea in such wretched weather, but there was no other choice. Sigurd mulled over their options with his companions, weighing the dangers and the possible outcomes. "I think we ought to seek refuge either in Wessex or Northumberland, or perhaps try and make our way to Flanders and travel overland to Denmark. The north of England might offer us respite from Beornwulf's scanty power, especially since there are plenty of Vikings there," he mused. "Then let's ride out to the north, and hire more men if we can. We can set our sights on Denmark or Flanders afterwards," one of them decided. With that, they set their course. Sigurd had hoped to take the captive ship along with them, but they lacked the manpower to handle both vessels if things went awry. So they hugged the coastline of East Anglia, then turned and went north, past the treacherous waters of the Wash, and made it to the Humber River. The weather was bitterly cold all the way, but they were able to avoid any nasty squalls. Just before they reached the Humber, they made a pit stop at a small river to replenish their water supplies. There were no houses in sight, so Sigurd and Freyja decided to head ashore to stretch their legs while the water casks were being filled. "It feels good to be back on solid ground, Sigurd," exclaimed Freyja, after she'd trounced him up a small hillock. "I've been at sea for so long that I barely feel any different," chuckled Sigurd, spreading his fur cloak on the snow for Freyja to perch on. As they sat there catching their breath, gazing out over the wide swathes of land, dotted with wooded glades and forests that reached far inland, they heard the unmistakable hoot of a war horn coming from the direction of the ships. "Come on, Freyja!" shouted Sigurd, leaping up from the ground, "something's not right on the ships!"

Chapter 13

LEOFRIC OF WESSEX

They raced down the hill and soon emerged from the trees onto the riverbank. Biorn was already gathering his men. "What's the matter, Biorn?" Haldor asked. "I'm not sure, but look up the ice there," Biorn replied. He pointed towards the frozen bed of the small river, and Sigurd saw a large group of armed men running towards them, pulling a sledge. Sigurd observed them carefully for a moment. "I don't think they intend to attack us, Biorn. Otherwise, they wouldn't have a sledge. They appear to be Saxons, so let's be prepared," Sigurd responded. As more men arrived from the ships, the Saxons approached. When they saw the Northmen waiting for them, they stopped running. A well-dressed man in a bearskin mantle and helmet rushed forward. Freyja exclaimed, "Sigurd, he's not older than you! And you were afraid of him!" Sigurd did not respond, but smiled, as the Saxon was just a young man, although a noble-looking one. He was almost as tall as Sigurd but not as wide, with an honest face that immediately caught Haldor's attention. "Are you Danes or Norsemen?" the stranger asked. "Norsemen," Sigurd answered. "And you're Saxons, I presume." "Quite right," the boy laughed, glancing over his shoulder. "Are you plundering the country?" "No," Sigurd replied. "We're Christians. Tell your men to stand back, for our arrows are nearly drawn." The boy laughed again as if it were a joke. He turned and waved to his men, and they stopped.

"Let me explain," he said. "I'm Leofric, Haldor Alfric's son from Wessex, and this is my sister Sigrid. In short, we're fleeing from King Beornwulf's men. Will you help us?" Suspecting a trap, Sigurd stared at the boy intently, but the youth met his gaze straight on, and Sigurd's suspicions vanished. "Where is your sister, and where are your pursuers?" he asked. Leofric pointed to the sledge. "My sister is unwell, and we had to carry her." Suddenly, his face grew serious. "Please, sir Norseman, hurry with your answer for God's sake! The king's men are less than half a mile behind us, and there are almost sixty of them, while half of ours are wounded or sick."

Sigurd emerged and firmly gripped the hand of the person before him. "No time for idle chatter! Get your sister and the sick or injured men onto my ships and let all your warriors join mine. Freyja, take charge of him and prepare the boats immediately," Sigurd commanded. The young man called forth his squad, dividing them as Sigurd had ordered and mobilizing 20 Saxons to join the Norsemen. "We will teach Beornwulf's fighters a harsh lesson, Biorn. Distribute the troops as you see fit," said the young man. One hundred fifty feet ahead was a bend in the river, and Biorn signaled for his men to conceal themselves behind the dry bushes that lined the banks while he went to scout ahead. Moments later, he came rushing back full tilt shouting, "They're here! Hold on until they're alongside us, then unleash arrows and axes upon them!" Before long, the pursuing party of sixty Saxons led by two commanders appeared. "Take out the leaders, men," Sigurd whispered. As the group came between the two bands of Norsemen, Biorn's horn sounded and a wave of arrows rained down upon the compact formation of Saxons. Simultaneously, the Vikings drew their swords and axes and charged forward. Although the Saxons put up a valiant defense, their leaders fell at the first attack. After a fierce minute of hand-to-hand fighting, the Saxons faltered and fled. Sigurd had led his men, locking swords in a duel with a tall Saxon. The latter wounded Sigurd severely in the shoulder during the first exchange of blows. Dropping his shield, Sigurd wielded his excellent sword with both hands, charging forth towards his opponent. His first blow made the other's shield-arm go numb with shock; the second made his sword fly out of his hand, and he fell heavily on the ice. Seeing that the enemy was broken, Sigurd paused and yelled aloud, "Retreat, men, retreat! Our goal is not to slaughter them, but to teach them a lesson!" While his Norse warriors obediently fell back, Leofric's Saxons pursued the fleeing Saxons, and Sigurd couldn't really blame them. Then he turned to his fallen opponent, who lay there looking up at him, waiting for the killing blow. "Get up," Sigurd chuckled. "I'm not a murderer!"

The Saxon slowly rose to his feet with a look of amazement on his face. He took Sigurd's hand in his own and knelt down, kissing it in gratitude. "Thanks, lord," he spoke, "you are the first to ever defeat Wulf in swordplay. If you are willing to accept him, he will serve you faithfully!" Sigurd responded with a faint smile, but Biorn quickly caught him when he suddenly lost consciousness. Blood streamed from his wounded shoulder, and he was quickly losing strength. Biorn held him tightly as Wulf removed his woolen tunic and efficiently bandaged the wound. Biorn watched with suspicion, but soon he and Wulf carried Sigurd back to shore. As they drew closer, Freya ran up to them in a panic. "Sigurd! Is Sigurd okay?" Biorn reassured her, stating that his wound was minor and that he would be back on his feet in no time. Wulf, the one responsible for Sigurd's injury, surprised Biorn with his tenderness. He carefully placed Sigurd against an ice-hummock and washed his face with snow until he slowly regained consciousness. "You rest now," Biorn instructed as he rose, "I will take care of the embarking." By the time the water casks were loaded, Leofric and the Saxons had returned and even the Saxon boy showed remorse for what had happened. All the men were divided between the two ships: the Jomsvikings, Thorstein's courtmen, a dozen Saxons on the "Crane" and thirty Saxons and Norse prisoners on the other. The sails were raised, and the ships set course eastward, leaving the shore behind. Sigurd sat at the front of the "Crane" with Freya and the two Saxons beside him. "Tell me your story," he requested, introducing himself and Freya. "Our father was the Haldor of Wessex," began Leofric, "but King

Beornwulf was jealous of his popularity, and relentlessly persecuted him. Three weeks ago, armed men came to seize our father, but he escaped to a Danish ship on the coast. But my elder brother, Alfgar, was taken and blinded." Freyja and Sigurd gasped in horror, unable to comprehend such cruelty. But Leofric only smiled sadly, knowing the extent of the King's barbarity. "You do not know what Beornwulf is capable of. In his eyes, Alfgar is as good as dead, as he is unfit to become Haldor in his current condition."

"My father had just enough time to send a messenger to warn us in Lincoln. We fled just in time to make it to the fens and escape. Eighty men, all loyal servants of my father, came with us. We fought off Beornwulf's men twice, but wounds and sickness took their toll on my men. These are the only ones left. Last week, Sigrid fell ill with a fever and we had to flee again. But thanks to Haldor Sigurd, we are now safe. We will never forget that we owe you our lives, Haldor Sigurd!" Freyja took charge of the sick girl immediately. Thanks to his temperate lifestyle, Sigurd's wound was beginning to heal quickly, and Wulf was proving to be an invaluable asset. He had been educated in a monastery and was skilled in the art of healing. He was also devoted to the boy Haldor. "I thought I would be killed immediately," Wulf told Sigurd, who had summoned him. "You're the best swordsman and the only merciful Viking I've ever met. My life is yours, Haldor, if you'll have it." Wulf's words were so sincere that Sigurd gladly accepted his offer. Wulf was an expert swordsman as well as a leech, and he could read and write, which was no small accomplishment. They held a council on the "Crane's" forecastle to decide on their next move. They finally agreed to run south and cross to Flanders where Leofric and Sigrid would likely find their father. As soon as they made their decision, Biorn took charge of the other vessel (which has been given the name "Snake") and they set sail that evening. Luckily they did because a gale swept down from the northeast during the night and left them helpless before it. The Saxons on board the "Snake," most of whom had never been to sea before, were of little use. Even Leofric was sick, though Sigrid was spared. However, there was nothing they could do except ride out the storm and keep the ships before the wind. It was bitterly cold, but since the Norsemen weren't bothered by it much and the girls were bundled up, there was no great suffering.

Sigurd felt confident in the two ships. They were new and could handle the rough, unpredictable waves with ease. Unlike traditional Viking ships, they could only sail with a fair wind or a wind from the side. The crew of four discussed their situation that evening in the cramped quarters of the "Crane's" cabin. Sigurd laughed and shook off the snow as he entered, "We're certainly getting all the storms we want, Freyja. Should we take our chances and head around to the southern end of England?" Leofric quickly opposed, "No! Can't we make for Normandy? Many Vikings are there, and it's settled by Norsemen." Sigurd shook his head, "Not unless the wind shifts." Freyja chimed in, "I see you're thinking about getting me back home. While I'd love to see Vendland again, it's best if we just take the simplest course. Run before the wind, then around England and back to King Thorstein." Sigurd chuckled, "It does sound easy. I'd do it if I were alone, but with you and Sigrid on board, I don't want to take any unnecessary risks." Sigrid laughed too as Leofric, overcome by seasickness, left the cabin. "Don't mind us, Haldor. Head for Ireland by all means!" Sigurd replied, "We'll see how things look in the morning. I'm turning in now to get some sleep."

Chapter 14

IN BRETSCADE

The morning broke dark and gloomy, with no land in sight. Sigurd, concluding that they had been driven below the Thames if not below the end of England, ordered the helmsman to steer due west, and while he was unable to communicate with the "Snake," he saw Biorn follow his example at once, and knew that he understood. The gale had now lessened to a steady wind from the northeast, interspersed with flurries of snow, and both ships drove steadily along under half-canvas. For two days they held this course, and then Sigurd held a shouted conference with Biorn. It seemed evident that they had been carried south of England, so the prows were turned north, and the next morning land appeared. Leofric had found his sea legs by this time, while Sigrid was rapidly gaining strength and color from the salt sea air, which drove the marsh fever out of her. She was a very pretty girl, indeed, with her blue eyes and long flaxen hair, and she and Freyja were firm friends from the start. Wulf, who was now more a friend than a captive, was a great favorite with all on board, even with Leofric's Saxons. On the morning that land was sighted, he drew Sigurd aside. "Haldor, we must have fresh water at once. Three of the casks were loosened by the storm and have run out; there is only a cask or two of ale left." Sigurd made a wry face. "Well, that will keep us from thirst, and the men like it well enough, though I have little taste for it; but perhaps we can get water from some river along the coast here, or from the 'Snake.'" Wulf disagreed. "All Beornwulf's Jarls and Thanes will be looking for us, you may be sure, and as

soon as we are sighted the housecarls will be poured down wherever we land."
Sigurd thought it over, and finally signaled the "Snake." Biorn drew alongside,
but when Sigurd mentioned the shortness of water, the old Viking gave a cry of
dismay. "Why, we thought to get some from you! Never mind, we are drawing
into the coast, and I will make a landing and find out where we are. We cannot be
very far from South Wales, and once there it will be plain sailing, for the people
there are of my own race, and I have not forgotten the language of the Cymry."

They sailed towards the rocky shore for hours before discovering a frozen
bay with a small village perched atop a cliff. Leofric guessed they were likely
fishermen, but without a nearby river, they would have to melt some ice. Biorn's

ship carefully pushed through the outer edge of ice, and after testing it with oars, he and a dozen men made it to shore. The villagers were frightened of the pirates, but Biorn quickly calmed their fears by buying a large quantity of fish. Returning to the ships, Biorn reported that there was no fresh water, but the villagers melted ice for their needs. Haldor suggested that they continue towards North Wales, even though there wouldn't be much help from the locals on the coast. When asked how long it would take to reach North Wales, Biorn replied they would get there the following night or the day after at the latest. After loading a supply of ice, they hoisted their sails and moved at full speed to avoid getting caught in another storm. The following morning, they reached Land's End and turned their prows north. By nightfall, they could see land ahead, and early next morning, they drew close to the shore. Biorn believed he knew where they were and led the way, promising to quickly find an open river.

Before noon on that day, a great cry of excitement erupted from the men as they laid their eyes upon a bay that stretched out before them. A river meandered down through it, though it was a treacherous path for ships as the ice threatened to seal them in from either side. Yet, the courageous crew of the "Crane" followed close behind the "Snake" and navigated the narrow channel with ease. A half mile up, the band of brothers encountered a most unexpected sight. Whooping to herald his arrival, Biorn then started sounding his war horn, prompting Sigurd to raise the alarm and prepare his men for the worst. Leofric, in haste, fastened his armor together and partnered with Sigurd as the "Snake" rounded the bend. There, the men were met with the sight of two imposing ships nestled into the shore, preparing for winter, and a camp nearby. From their appearance and habits, it was apparent that these were the Danes. Also visible from afar was a town with a sizable population atop a neighboring hill. As the "Crane" came alongside the "Snake," Sigurd saw that the warriors on shore had begun to arm themselves and stand guard around the ships. Biorn identified the town as Neath and revealed that in the distant past, the place used to be his home. Asking for Sigurd's counsel on the matter at hand, Biorn suggested that they hail the Neath ships and determine their intent. Agreeing with Biorn's intuition,

Sigurd instructed his men to draw as close as they could to the shore. The vessel stopped at about two to three hundred yards from the beach, as the ice made it impossible for it to move closer. Soon following their call, a dozen men from the Neath ships started walking over the ice toward the "Crane." As they neared the vessel, Freyja, a member of Sigurd's protective cadre, let out a shriek and snatched Sigurd's arm. "Oh, Fairhair, look at that big man in front! That is Halfdan, the brother of Queen Gunhild, and my own uncle!" she cried. Sigurd gazed upon Halfdan and recalled the time he had spent observing the man on King Harald's court while Freyja explained their family connection. Halfdan stopped just before reaching a spear that had been cast and called out, "Who are you, and do you come in peace or war?"

Sigurd burst out laughing. "You don't recognize your friends, Haldor?" he joked. Haldor turned sharply and surveyed the ship before running towards them. "Sigurd Fairhair!" he exclaimed as he got closer. "And by the eye of Odin! Is that Freyja?" Freyja beamed and jumped down onto the ice, throwing her arms around her uncle's neck. He struggled to disengage himself while mockingly shouting, "Help! Help! Are you trying to make me a captive? Let loose! Respect my dignity!" Sigurd followed Freyja onto the ice and clasped Haldor's hand. Freyja joked, "Be careful, uncle. Sigurd is your equal in dignity now!" Sigurd nodded at the surprised look on Haldor's face. "Yes, I am one of Thorstein Tryggveson's men now, Haldor. He recently made me a Haldor, although I am too young for such an honor." "Nonsense, nonsense!" Haldor replied, his eyes gleaming with happiness. "You are the handsomest Haldor I have ever seen in my life, upon my word! But come up to the camp." "Wait," Sigurd said, turning to his ships. "Leofric and Sigrid, join us. Wulf and Biorn, take charge of the ships and lay them up on the shore, beside the others. We are with friends." As Leofric and Sigrid climbed down to the ice, the young Haldor introduced them to his uncle, who greeted them warmly. "I have heard of your father's misfortune," he exclaimed. "I fought against him three or four years ago, and he was a noble foeman. However, he is safe in Flanders now and is likely to return before long." Leofric was surprised. "What do you mean?" "Come along to the camp, and I'll tell you." Haldor led the way to the shore. "It's too cold to be standing out here talking." As they entered the camp, the news of the Jomsvikings' arrival spread quickly, and loud blasts went up from the horns. The Danes met them with shouts of joy, for the men of Jomsborg were prime favorites with King Harald's men. Sigurd found several he knew, while Freyja was met with fresh cheers. As they entered the large hut of Halfdan, the Haldor drove the men off.

"Get out of here!" Halfdan cried, shooing the rowdy crew away from his doorstep. "Go help stow the ships up onshore. We have much to discuss and need some peace and quiet!" With a boisterous cheer, the men tumbled away, leaving Halfdan to close the door with a sigh of relief. "Welcome, friends!" he said to the newcomers, offering food and water. "You must be hungry after your journey." Sigurd, the group's leader, thanked him and asked how he ended up in Wales. Halfdan explained how he was sent by Harald to make arrangements with the Welsh king, Idwal ap Meirig, to join them in their upcoming battles. "I've been here for a few months now, and King Idwal is on board," Halfdan said. "We see him almost every day. But first, let's get comfortable." He piled furs for the two women, Freyja and Sigrid, while he and the boys sat on a long wooden bench. As they chatted, Halfdan couldn't help but remark on the strange and barbaric-sounding Welsh names. Sigrid joked that the Welsh probably found their own names just as harsh, and it was all a matter of perspective. Eventually, Sigurd finished recounting his tale, and Halfdan showed the group to their makeshift lodgings for the night. His own hut would be shared with the boys, while the two women would have a separate one. With their beds prepared, Halfdan bid them goodnight and left to attend to his duties as a messenger of Harald and a strategist in the upcoming battles.

Chapter 15

IN WINTER QUARTERS

The following day, Halfdan's group merged with the newcomers and worked together to bring the two ships onto the shore. Disassembling and unloading the vessels, they utilized parties of men to scavenge the surrounding forests for firewood and timber to construct fresh huts. By evening, a hundred and fifty men accomplished the task, and they rested peacefully for several days, allowing time for those that were wounded or sick to recover. Sigrid recovered almost entirely thanks to Halfdan's cheerfulness and rough humor. Sigurd and Leofric desired to explore the nearby town and locate suitable accommodation, yet Halfdan advised them otherwise, warning of King Idwal's watchful eye. The Welsh king was suspicious of any Northman within a hundred miles, and with good cause, considering Bretscade's terrible ravaging by the Vikings. Halfdan reminded them of Biorn's youth when Vikings kidnapped him. Furthermore, the town did not offer much worth visiting, only a castle and a few shabby homes. King Idwal forbade their men from entering the area. On occasion, country folk came down to the camp with their market wares, providing fresh meat and food, making it an impromptu marketplace. The Vikings' camp became a fair during these times. The Welsh people were different; small with their bright quick eyes and black straight hair. Their looks contrasted strikingly with the light-haired Northmen and Saxons.

Sigurd and Leofric were initially worried about how the Saxons and Danes would get along because the two groups had always been sworn enemies. Happily, their concerns turned out to be unfounded. Halfdan learned from the locals that wolves were wreaking havoc in the nearby forests, so the group fashioned skis, and even Sigrid learned how to use the "snow skates," as the Saxons called them, to travel through the snow. On the second week of their stay, they decided to go on a three-day wolf hunt, leaving Biorn in charge of the camp. Upon their return, Biorn informed them that King Idwal planned to visit them the next day with his entire court. The group sprang into action, decorating their huts with pine boughs from the forest, and hanging tapestries and cloths that Sigurd found in Biorn's captured cargo in Halfdan's large hut. They polished their armor and weapons and formed three divisions: the Danes, Norsemen, and Saxons, clustering together under the standards of Halfdan, Sigurd, and Leofric. When the Welsh were spied winding down the hill towards the camp, the Vikings sounded their horns in greeting. Leading the procession was a group of archers, with the King and his court on small, shaggy ponies following behind. Idwal was larger than most of his followers, with sharp black eyes and a strong chin shaved with two long mustaches in the Danish fashion. As he approached, Halfdan met him and offered his greetings. "Welcome, my lord King!" he exclaimed. "We are pleased to return the hospitality of your castle!" Idwal grinned. "Indeed, Haldor. I am relieved to see that your men have no intention of raiding my borders. We would have a tough time repelling such a force as yours. I heard you had brought in a fresh band of Vikings, so I came down to make sure we were not in any danger."

Halfdan made a gesture to Sigurd and his companions, indicating for them to approach. As they did, Halfdan turned his attention to the Saxon, Leofric, and examined him and his group of friends with furrowed brows. "It has been many a year since a Saxon came seeking refuge among us Cymry," the king remarked. Leofric then proceeded to tell his tale, and the king's expression softened. "To be honest, I have no love for the Saxons," he admitted, "but as long as you are enemies of Beornwulf, that changes things. Tell me, if your father were to return home and I joined forces with King Harald, would you fight for or against me?" The king's gaze bore into Leofric, but the young man met his stare head-on, a smile playing at his lips. "My lord King, I would fight for my home against any invader. However, should my father choose to join King Harald, I would march at his side." Halfdan broke in with a chuckle. "Fear not, my lord. This Saxon will not pose a threat for some time to come. I'm sure that if we make a move against Beornwulf this spring, he will stand as strongly by our side as any of our nobles. But come, let us enter the camp." The Vikings parted to allow Idwal and his men to enter. Inside, Halfdan had arranged a banquet area in a cleared space, with long tables draped in a large sail, and a dozen fires blazing on either side. "By my faith!" exclaimed King Idwal. "This is a proper feast, Haldor! A banquet in the open air is much to my liking, and these fires would warm even an army!" As he spoke, the king shrugged off his fur cloak, revealing a light suit of armor beneath. He was accompanied by around forty nobles and a bishop whom Halfdan granted the place of honor. Amongst the Welsh, bishops, and priests were held in higher esteem than even the king himself. The group found the bishop to be a learned, kind, and deeply religious man. He took great interest in Freyja and Wulf, conversing with them both at length.

Halfdan had hunted for three days straight prior to the feast, as his venison supplies were running low. The Vikings had caught some large fish from the river and presented a Saxon-style boar's head to the Welshmen. They worked tirelessly to create an exceptional feast, and Bishop Dafydd's presence kept the revelry under control. As per tradition, there was an exchange of gifts before the King departed. Biorn and Haldor Halfdan, the skilled smiths, had created a beautiful byrnie of woven gold rings which the King was delighted to receive. He gifted Halfdan with a great boar hound and Sigurd with a fur-edged cloak embroidered in silver thread. As he knew of the two girls' presence, he also thoughtfully brought new outfits suited to their rank. Idwal's bond with the Vikings was strengthened, and he pledged to unite with them in their quest as soon as King Harald landed in the east, pouring his men into the West Saxon earldoms. Halfdan was certain that the Danish king would fulfill his oath, which he had sworn at his accession feast. The camp settled down for the rest of the winter, with hunting parties on skis bringing in fresh meat each week from the surrounding forests. The smiths repaired and augmented their weaponry while the chiefs of the Northmen crafted their armor. Sigurd's work at the forge fortified him and broadened his shoulders significantly. The two girls relished their time in the camp as every man adored them. They joined in the hunting parties, with Freyja taking down many a wolf with her bow while Sigrid, less of a warrior, still got involved with the same enthusiasm. Time passed quickly, and by March, the snow had melted, and the four ships underwent a thorough overhaul. They were freshly caulked and pitched, masts erected, and finally, they were ready to sail again, lying at anchor.

King Idwal made a return trip to the camp, and the chiefs accompanied him back to the castle for a brief stay. He generously provided provisions of all sorts for the ships, and come April, Sigurd bade farewell to Halfdan. On the eve of their departure, they gathered inside Haldor's hut. "Now, Haldor," said Sigurd, "I presume you'll be taking Freyja home with you?" "That remains to be seen," Halfdan replied teasingly, "depending on whether or not she wants to go. She seems to rather enjoy drifting about the world, relying on a gallant knight to rescue and safeguard her from danger!" Freyja blushed, "That's not fair, Uncle! I will be going home with you. But listen, why don't you come with us to King Thorstein's and return via the northern route? It's just as swift that way and less perilous too!" The towering Haldor sprang to his feet, "Hurrah! I never expected that! I had intended to journey home via the southern coast of England, but the truth is, this way is just as fast and I am keen on meeting this King Thorstein whom you speak so highly of." It was all arranged that Halfdan would not set sail till the following week, so he rushed to gather his chiefs. He explained the new strategy, and by torchlight, the men worked on and completed the loading of his two ships. By morning, everything was set. With the wind in their favor, they sailed out toward the bay. After a few days of coasting along the Irish shore, they finally caught sight of the stunning towers of Dublin.

Chapter 16

AN AMBUSCADE

Sigurd's return to the court of King Thorstein was met with immense joy, as he had been feared lost in a coastal storm before his departure. Halfdan, on the other hand, spent only a week in Dublin before deciding to make his way back home without any further delay. As Sigurd said farewell to Freyja, he couldn't help but feel sorrowful. They had grown very close during their travels. Although Leofric and Sigrid remained with him, he knew he would miss her greatly. "Never mind," he promised. "We'll land in Norway this summer or fall, and I'll make sure to turn up at the Danish court, or in Vendland, shortly after." "I'll be happy to see Vidar again when I get home," Freyja replied. "It'll almost be as good as seeing you." Halfdan had informed them of Vidar's safe arrival back home, meaning that Haldor Eirik had stayed true to his word. Sigurd and Leofric accompanied Halfdan's ships for a few miles in their vessel, the "Crane," before bidding farewell to Freyja and turning back towards Dublin. Sigurd's duties at the court were light, as there were no Jarls ruling over the Irish kingdom like there were in Norway. All he had to do was command the courtmen. Leofric, meanwhile, refused to do homage to King Thorstein, as he remained loyal to his own land. However, the King still gave him a command, and Leofric proved himself to be a capable leader. At the start of summer, King Thorstein took all his warships out of the water, scraped the bottoms, and gave them a thorough overhaul. Thorir Klakke, who was still in Dublin, urged the King to set sail for Norway as soon as possible, claiming that bonders would flock to him upon his arrival and that he need not bring a large force. Thorstein understood very well that Thorir was not to be trusted, but he kept it to himself. Later, he confided in Sigurd that Thorir was someone who deserved to be hanged. While Sigurd was away in England, two half-brothers of King Thorstein's had been driven from Norway by Haldor Ragnvald and sought refuge with the King in Ireland. Thorir tried to bribe them, but luckily they pretended to agree with him while revealing his plans.

Haldor Ragnvald had sent him there but the King didn't seem too happy about it. With a grim smile he warned, "Thorir will try to kill me on the voyage, but if he fails, Ragnvald has men waiting for me at a certain point on shore. They are instructed to take me out. Permanently." Sigurd was outraged, and even the priest Thangbrand growled, "Let me handle him, Thorstein! I guarantee he won't be bothering you again!" Thorstein laughed heartily, "Thangbrand, you're better suited for being a Viking than a priest! If I ever conquer Norway, I shall send you to Iceland to spread Christianity!" The priest's face lit up at the prospect. "Thank you, my king! It's a shame that such a beautiful island has no churches of Christ. Even if I face resistance, I can handle it." Sigurd laughed at the mixture of warrior and priest in Thangbrand who had joined forces with Thorstein after being forced out of his home. Although he was deeply religious, it was clear that he was also an ideal candidate to bring Christianity to heathen Iceland. At that time, conversion was a bloody business, and the Cross and sword went hand in hand in spreading the faith. The old gods of Norway had many martyrs to their name before Christianity prevailed in later years. Around Dublin, irregular fighting occurred. The Irish kings were constantly trying to reclaim their land from the Norsemen, but were always outgunned by the well-armed Vikings. Thorstein had no problems maintaining law and order for several miles around the city. One day, Thorstein asked Sigurd, "How would you like to visit King Brian Boroimhe? I want to make peace with him before I leave Dublin for Norway. I cannot depend on my brother and want to ensure that Dublin is safe for at least a year."

"I would be delighted," responded Sigurd, "for I have heard so many tales about the wonders of Ireland's interior that I long to see it with my own eyes." "Very well," replied the King. "I will have letters written in Irish and you can bring along whomever you wish, along with an interpreter. Be ready to leave on Monday, as I believe the King should be in Kells, a large city about thirty miles to the west. I will provide a trustworthy guide." Thangbrand, the priest, heard about Sigurd's journey and eagerly requested to join him, which was granted graciously by Thorstein. And so, on Monday morning, Sigurd, Thangbrand, and twenty men left Dublin. Their weapons were secured peacefully and they brought along an Irish captive as their guide and interpreter, who promised to guide them to Kells in exchange for his freedom. Sigurd laughed when he saw the priest join them. Thangbrand was wearing a byrnie beneath his robe, a lightweight steel cap on his head, and had a shield and sword attached to his saddle bow. "No one knows what could happen," he responded bravely to Sigurd's laughter. "We may be ambushed by these Irish robbers, or the guide may lead us astray. It's best to be prepared for anything." After a brisk journey, they arrived at the boundary of Thorstein's territory and then traversed through woods and swamps for about twelve miles. As evening approached, they found themselves at an open plain, which was partially cultivated. The spires and towers of a grand city stood out in the distance. Several times, they were stopped by groups of Irishmen, but their guide remained faithful. Sigurd was amazed by the sight of Kells. "This is marvelous!" he exclaimed. "I had no idea that such civilization existed so close to Dublin!" Thangbrand chuckled. "Kells rarely falls prey to Viking raids in recent years. It's a fortified city, with an impressive monastery within its walls. I've been here once before and discovered that it's a beautiful land in peacetime, but in war, it's nearly impossible to reach the city." As they approached, Sigurd saw that this was true since defense systems lined either side of the road, and he discovered several stone castles as well. Just as the sun began to set, they entered the gates of Kells, and their guide rushed ahead to arrange lodging for the men.

As they made their way through the streets, they were met with scowls and curses from the Irish. The Northmen had given them good reason to hate, having ravaged their lands, destroyed their monasteries, and wreaked havoc upon their once splendid civilization. Had it not been for King Brian's strong hand, they surely would have taken over the entire country. That evening, they took up lodging at a grand inn, and the following morning they made their way to the court. King Brian's palace was beyond anything Sigurd had ever seen, even in London. It was built of stone, and the great hall was adorned with an array of arms and tapestries. The nobles that filled the room were dressed much like the Northmen, but their golden bracelets and cloak-pins were richly crafted, with the precious metal abounding. Sigurd led his men to the high-seat and bowed low to King Brian, a powerful and stern-faced man. He was in his sixties and opened and read the letters from Thorstein with a frown, then handed them to a monk who stood at his side. "Sir Haldor," he said, without rising, as he fixed his gray eyes on Sigurd. "I will have an answer written at once. For now, you and your men will stay in my palace here. King Thorstein is a brave and worthy man, and I am pleased to conclude a year's truce with him. If all Northmen were like him, Erin would be a happier land." The monk translated the King's words, and Sigurd withdrew, bowing low. Thangbrand then headed to the monastery, bringing Sigurd along. The monks were somewhat surprised at the warlike appearance of the priest but entertained them well nonetheless, showing them around the grounds. The next morning, King Brian summoned Sigurd once more. He handed him a parchment for King Thorstein and awarded him a heavy golden arm-ring. The Norsemen quickly departed from the city, making their way back to Thorstein's territory at a good pace. As they reached the borders, Sigurd and Thangbrand rode ahead of the party. Thangbrand, an adept horseman, showed Sigurd how to make his steed curvet and prance, and as they continued, they eventually outpaced the rest of the group.

They rounded a curve in the path, twisting below a dense canopy of trees. Suddenly, several men leaped towards their mounts, attempting to seize them by the reins. Meanwhile, others charged at Sigurd and Thangbrand, trying to wrench them from their saddles. Although they struggled to retrieve their weapons, attackers descended from the treetops and overwhelmed them. Within moments, the two Vikings were tightly bound, helpless and dragged off into the inky depths of the forest.

Chapter 17

THORKEL TURNS UP

In the distance, faint shouts and the sound of horns trailed behind them as the group moved on from where their leaders had been ambushed. Eventually, it became silent. Sigurd noticed that they were being transported by a band of two dozen Irishmen who were making their way north through the forest. He started to say something to the priest at his side, but one of their captors forcefully struck him on the mouth, speaking sharply in Irish. Sigurd stopped talking. As darkness fell, the group stopped beside a stream. Sigurd guessed they had traveled several miles from where they were taken. A fire was started, where the Irishmen cooked their meal. The two prisoners were flung down beneath a large tree. "What foolishness to leave our guide," grumbled Thangbrand, his thick black beard covering most of his face. "I wish they would give us food." Their wish was granted, as the leader of the group approached them, cutting their ropes, giving them bread and meat, and a horn of water from the stream. But soon after, they were bound again. "They seem to be waiting for someone," Sigurd exclaimed. "Did you see the leader send men out in all directions?" Indeed, the leader had sent men out as soon as they had arrived, and an hour later, a second group of men emerged into the firelight with a shout. Sigurd cried out in surprise as he recognized Thorkel Gormson at the front, whom he had left in London the previous winter. The new arrivals were also Irishmen, except for Thorkel. The leader of the original group welcomed Thorkel and, to Sigurd's surprise, Thorkel handed him a bag that jingled pleasantly. Thorkel then stepped forward to Sigurd's side. "So, I finally have you, Lord Haldor!" he exclaimed, his dark eyes filled with malice. "It's quite a distance from London to Ireland, but I have waited and watched patiently." "It's a pity that I didn't hit you harder that night," retorted Sigurd. "What is your objective with this attack?" Thorkel laughed harshly. "You're going with me to Haldor Ragnvald, my dear fellow. As for this follower of the White Christ, I think I'll hand him over to my friends in the morning."

Sigurd paled, aware that any Norsemen caught by the Irish would face a gruesome fate. Thangbrand, however, defiantly yelled, "Release me, traitor, and face me with blade in hand!" Thorkel scoffed, "I thought followers of your God were docile and submissive, willing to die for their beliefs." Thangbrand reddened with shame and let out no further retort. Thorkel then turned his back, posted guards, and soon the group slumbered peacefully under the tree cover. Though the Norsemen had not been stripped of their weapons, their bindings left them useless. Sigurd, however, noticed his sword's peace tie had been ripped off in the forest's rush. An hour later, Thangbrand nudged Sigurd's hand with his own. Lying side by side, unbound, and with a snoozing guard a few feet away, Thangbrand gestured to the sheathed sword. Sigurd cautiously rolled on his stomach and edged the weapon close enough for the priest. Thangbrand faced the other way and his groping fingers finally met the hilt. Just in time, the guard strolled over to check on the sleepers, and Sigurd heard a barely audible noise when Thangbrand cut his bonds. When the sentry hovered over Sigurd to ensure everything was still in place, Thangbrand quickly overpowered the unsuspecting guard. Swiftly muzzling and capturing the sentry, Thangbrand then freed Sigurd, whispering through his own stiff lips, "If only my hands weren't so numb, I'd have done better." Still struggling with their own numbness, the companions broke free and Thangbrand questioned, "which way, Haldor?" "Westerly, Thangbrand," answered Haldor. "Once we encounter any of King Brian's men, we'll be safe. He has a bracelet recognizable in these parts and you are a priest, which will both prove helpful."

Silently, Sigurd and Thangbrand gathered their shields from the sleeping men and slipped away into the inky darkness of the forest. The moon was rising, casting a pale glow on their path, giving them just enough light to move quickly. They ran for what seemed like an eternity, the trees blurring past them. Sigurd knew they had to move quickly, navigate the rough terrain, and put as much distance between themselves and their pursuers as possible. Finally, after what felt like hours, Thangbrand signaled for a break. They both collapsed, gasping for air. Thangbrand was panting heavily, and Sigurd knew he couldn't keep up the pace much longer. As they caught their breath, Sigurd wondered if they would be pursued. Thangbrand was resolute, gritting his teeth and promising to fight to the death rather than fall into their hands. They continued on, taking turns walking and running. As the first light of dawn broke through the trees, they saw that the forest was thinning out, giving way to cultivated fields. They hoped they were getting closer to safety. A faint yell rang out behind them, and Sigurd knew that they were not alone. They had to pick up their pace, running for their lives. Thangbrand was running out of energy, but Sigurd refused to leave him behind. Finally, Thangbrand stopped, exhausted. "Go on, Fairhair," he said. "Your life is worth more than mine. I'll hold them off as long as I can." Sigurd hesitated for a moment, but he knew that Thangbrand was right. He had to get to safety, and he had to do it quickly. With a heavy heart, he ran on, hoping that his only friend in this strange land would somehow survive.

Sigurd spoke calmly, "One of the rules of Jomsborg is to never abandon a comrade." Thangbrand erupted, "Forget your Jomsborg rules! Go, and make haste!" Sigurd interjected, "Listen! Do you hear that horn?" In the distance, they could hear the faint sound of a war horn coming from the west, and from behind them, the sound of their pursuers drawing closer. "Quickly, Fairhair," Thangbrand commanded, drawing his sword. "Go and seek help while I hold them off!" Sigurd unsheathed his own sword and smiled at Thangbrand's generosity. "Enough of this foolishness," Sigurd said, though the excitement of battle coursed through him. "Let's take our stand by that massive oak tree where we can fight without fear of being attacked from behind." They positioned themselves on either side of the towering oak tree just as the first pursuer arrived. Within minutes, a circle of armed men surrounded them. Thorkel, the leader of the Irish, bravely led a charge of a dozen men straight towards the tree. The combat began with furious intensity. The Irish came at them with long knives, but were quickly repelled by the deadly blows of Thangbrand and Sigurd. As the Irish retreated, their chief ordered a barrage of arrows. Sigurd deflected one arrow with his shield and sliced the second arrow in half in mid-flight. The Irish onlookers were amazed by the display of precision and skill from the

Norsemen. Thangbrand replicated Sigurd's feat, but despite their efforts, they were eventually wounded by the onslaught of arrows. Suddenly, Thorkel leaped at Sigurd with a shout of impatience. The Irish circled around the combat with bated breath, observing every move, while Thangbrand protected Sigurd's back. Thorkel and Sigurd clashed blades three times, then, seeing an opening, Sigurd lunged forward, only to lose his footing on the dewy grass and fell headfirst onto the ground.

Thangbrand found himself on top of his enemy, towering over Thorkel. The Irish warriors, wielding their sharp knives, stood behind Thangbrand, waiting for an opportunity to strike. The priest engaged in a heated sword fight with Thorkel. Suddenly, Thorkel flung his arms up, disturbed by something flying past Thangbrand. A spear landed in Thorkel's body, and his followers screamed in horror. As Thangbrand glanced around, helping Sigurd stand up, he noticed King Brian Boroimhe sneaking up behind him, brandishing his own sword. The king's men were swarming the scene, chasing down the frightened enemy soldiers in all directions and taking no mercy in killing them.

Chapter 18

A MISSION FOR THE KING

Speaking in Latin, the King's voice boomed across the room. Thangbrand recognized the language. He had been traveling with the King's men and they had just returned after a recent mishap. The King was not pleased, but he greeted them warmly nonetheless. "We owe you our lives, my lord," Thangbrand replied, grateful for their safe return. "Strange words for a man of God, sir priest!" the King laughed. "But I see that your blade has done good service to Haldor Sigurd. Perhaps in these times, a priest must be a man of the world as well." Thangbrand shot a glance at Sigurd, who held up the King's unbroken letters. They were safe, and the King's men had returned to escort them to Kells. Sigurd was in a hurry to get back to Dublin, so the King granted him an escort of fifty men. As they rode through the land of Thorstein, Sigurd dismissed the Irish and they surged forward, eager to reach their destination. But as the city came into view, Sigurd was struck with dismay. Instead of the King's standard, a giant black banner floated ominously from the castle. Puzzled, they rode closer and discovered that the shops were all closed, and the whole city was shrouded in mourning. Without hesitation, Sigurd excused himself and hurried to the great hall. Inside, he found Thorstein sitting in the high seat, his head bowed low. Sigurd handed over the King's letters and asked, "Why is the black standard raised and why is the city in mourning?" Thorstein looked up slowly, his eyes heavy with sorrow. "Welcome back, Haldor, in an evil hour. Queen Gyda died last night." Sigurd was shocked by the news. The King slowly rose from his seat, approached Sigurd, and took his arm, saying, "Sigurd, come and talk to me. I am lonely, and the most wretched of all men."

As they paced up and down the hall, Thorstein confided in Sigurd about the tragic events of the previous night. The Queen had fallen ill, and despite the best efforts of Sigurd, a skilled healer, she still passed away. The King was consumed with grief and anger, asking why such an evil would befall him. Sigurd listened patiently to Thorstein's outburst, letting him express his pain. Then, in a soft voice, Sigurd reminded the King that it was the will of God. Perhaps this adversity was meant to test Thorstein's devotion to spreading the Word in heathen Norway. Thorstein knew this was true, but still found it hard to accept. He had been blessed with good fortune until now, and he struggled to bear the weight of this misfortune. However, he knew that if God wanted him to focus on spreading his gospel, then he had no choice but to obey. For many months, Thorstein was consumed by his grief over the loss of his beloved Queen. Two days later, she was laid to rest, and Thorstein threw himself into preparing for the expedition to Norway. It was a daunting task. Thorstein had a dozen warships in the harbor, but he couldn't take such a large force. In case he succeeded in Norway, Thorstein planned to leave his Irish land to his brother-in-law, Thorstein Kvaran, but he needed men to defend it. After consulting with Sigurd and his other chiefs, the King decided to take only the five largest ships which were designed to accommodate about seventy-five men each. Thorir Klakke, who had no idea that Thorstein was aware of his treacherous intentions, suggested that they launch a surprise attack on Haldor Ragnvald at Hlidskjalf before he could gather his men. Thorir hoped to kill Thorstein during the voyage, or that Ragnvald's men at Agdaness in Norway would eliminate Thorstein before he could put the plan into action.

Thorstein had a mission and that was to spread the Word of God to all who would listen. And as fate would have it, the Orkneys were in his path. It was there that he hoped to visit Haldor Sigurd, a powerful man whose fate could determine the success of Thorstein's expedition. As Thorstein's six ships sailed into Asmundar Bay, in Rognwald Island, they spotted a single ship at anchor. It was a sight to behold: the ship was magnificent, and its furnishings were fit for a king. Thorstein saw an opportunity and sent Sigurd Fairhair to fetch the commander of the ship, hoping to gather news about Norway. To his amazement, the commander turned out to be none other than Haldor Sigurd Lodvarson himself! Thorstein greeted him warmly, musing, "It seems Sigurds abound here! Yourself, my own Haldor Sigurd Fairhair, good Bishop Sigurd of England, and perhaps a score of my men, all sharing the same name." Haldor was unsure of Thorstein's intentions, not knowing where the king was headed or what he wanted. Thorstein urged Haldor to be baptized, but Haldor refused, stating that the faith of his fathers was enough for him. In response, Thorstein raised a sword in one hand and a cross in the other, making Haldor a proposal. "As the King of Norway, I claim all the lands that the Kings of Norway have possessed, including those you hold as Haldor of the Orkneys. You have two options: accept the true faith and be baptized along with your subjects, and I will let you keep the Jarldom you now possess and more importantly, you can hope to reign forevermore in a more magnificent kingdom than this. The second option is that you die, and after your death, I will come through the islands and help the people believe in the true God. Now, Haldor, it is your choice. Choose wisely." Haldor was caught in a dilemma, but he decided to make a choice. Slowly, he reached out for the cross that Thorstein held, and soon after, Bishop Sigurd baptized him. The crews celebrated with joyful shouts, and Haldor's fate was sealed, along with the fate of the Orkneys.

He pledged his loyalty to King Thorstein and surrendered his son, Hundi, who was also baptized, as a hostage on board Thorstein's vessel headed for Norway. The following day, Thorstein approached Sigurd with another urgent task that required a trusted and dependable messenger. "Sigurd," Thorstein addressed him. "Would you undertake yet another mission for me? You always manage to get by, no matter what the circumstance, and as this task holds particular importance, I can think of no one more qualified to handle it." Sigurd chuckled. "If I've made it through some precarious situations, Thorstein, it's not solely because of my own efforts. I've been lucky enough to have loyal companions, and for the rest, God has favored me. But tell me, what is this mission you speak of?"

Chapter 19

AT KING HARALD'S COURT

Freyja and Halfdan's voyage home to Denmark was safe and uneventful, but upon their arrival, they were greeted with a land much changed by the winter. The once-religious and peaceful Queen Gunhild had died, and without her restraining him, King Harald was preparing to invade England with his assembled forces. Freyja returned to the castle where she lived a solitary life. Her parents were long gone and her only company was her Uncle Halfdan. She found little joy in the presence of the moody and ambitious King Harald. However, when the King placed his two sons, Harald and Canute, under her care, she took great interest in their upbringing. The younger boy eventually grew up to become a great and worthy King of England, thanks largely to Freyja who had raised him well. As the summer progressed, men gathered and were dispatched to the Danish settlements in the northern regions of England to await the King's arrival in the fall. Halfdan was sent in command of one of these detachments, leaving Freyja even more alone than before. One day, King Harald summoned Freyja to the hall where he was surrounded by his chiefs. He informed her that the son of King Vladimir of Russia had sought her hand in marriage and that he had accepted the offer on her behalf. He explained that not only was it a great honor, but it would add a fleet of ships to his army from Russia. Freyja was overwhelmed by the news, but she responded bravely. She told the King that he had no right to dispose of her hand in this fashion. She also reminded him that she was not his subject and that her lands lay in Vendland. She even threatened to appeal to King Burislaf for protection from this outrage. The King's face darkened with anger, telling Freyja that she was to do as she was told. He reminded her that he was King and that even King Burislaf would do his bidding. He exclaimed that it was unheard of for a girl to make decisions with regard to her own marriage.

A low murmur of agreement echoed among the chiefs, causing Freyja to despair as she gazed desperately around the circle of fierce faces. She longed for her kind uncle to stand by her side, but as the King had pointed out, in those days a girl hardly had any say on whom she wanted to marry. It was the parents or guardians who decided and they did so without consulting the young woman. This left Freyja feeling helpless. "This is an honorable match," the King continued calmly, "so let's put an end to this protest. You will depart for Gardarike, Vladimir's capital, in two weeks with a suitable escort." With that, the girl was dismissed to her chambers. Young Canute, upon learning of the matter, tried to comfort her, but he was just as powerless as she was. Therefore, despite her resolution to never marry, even if she had to flee her home, the packing of her belongings proceeded. A week went by, and as Freyja sat sewing in the garden, a great commotion arose from the harbor. There were shouts and war horns mixed with the clashing of arms. She sent Canute to investigate. The boy returned not long after with his eyes shining and cheeks flushed with excitement. "Oh, Freyja!" he exclaimed. "We have guests! Two enormous ships just sailed into the harbor from a far-off land—the strangest ships! Instead of dragons in the bows, they had large, gilt crosses! All the men have shields adorned with red crosses, and when I saw them disembark, I saw fierce and mighty warriors among them!" Freyja turned pale upon hearing the news. What ships could these be, sailing beneath the Cross if not-? Canute continued excitedly: "And, Freyja, you must see their leaders! One old Viking was so fierce and audacious, and a dazzling young woman with bright golden hair, and a lad who must be her brother. But above them is a young man with hair like sunlight streaming over his shoulders and a magnificent golden helmet—" Freyja didn't stay to hear the rest. Abandoning her needlework, she raced toward her rooms, her heart pounding. Quickly summoning her handmaids, she adorned herself, then rushed to the deserted great hall. Dashing outside, she left the fortress and made her way to the harbor.

The town square was bustling with the locals and the castle's men, creating a path for Freyja to pass through. King Harald was amidst a group of people she couldn't see because of the swelling crowd. As she navigated through the throng, a familiar voice caught her ear, and suddenly, she was face to face with Sigurd Fairhair! "Freyja!" he exclaimed in delight. He then took her hands and held them tightly. "Sigurd!" she replied, noticing how much he had grown. "You've become a big man already! I'm so happy to see you, and I really need you too," she confided in a lower voice. Sigurd gave her a quick, concerned look, then turned to shout, "Here, Leofric, Sigrid!" Within moments, the two girls were embracing each other while the onlooking crowd stood by stunned. Sigurd recounted their entire tale to King Harald, who then ordered everyone to follow him to the castle. "Let's talk in peace there," he said. "Come up right away. My men will take care of your ships so your warriors can be entertained at the barracks." Sigurd left the arrangements to Biorn, and the four young friends followed King Harald to the castle. They settled in the hall below the high seat, where King Harald asked quite curiously, "Now, how in the world did you all end up here?" King Harald surely remembered Sigurd and was interested in their story. In return, Sigurd told him about Leofric and Sigrid's rescue. Harald nodded, "I know that story. Haldor Alfwic is with my army in England, even now. Please continue." "King Thorstein sent Leofric and his sister to you to request that they be taken to their father. If not that, then they were to be provided with a pilot who could take them safely to Flanders. But since you are planning on heading to England soon, that matter is settled," Sigurd continued. "I'll be overjoyed to have Haldor Alfwic's son with me," replied the King reassuringly. "They'll be safe until they reach Haldor." "As for myself," said Sigurd before he could finish, cries of amazement rung out from the Danes.

Harald leaped up, shouting, "King Thorstein has sailed for Norway? Skoal! Skoal!" The chiefs around him echoed his cheer. "He sent me to you, to ask that, if possible, you send him ships and men. Or, if you cannot do this, that at least you will not aid Haldor Ragnvald and Haldor Eirik," said Sigurd. "As for the first request, I cannot do that. I need every man I can raise. But be sure to let Thorstein know that he does not have to worry about an attack from me. I will be joyful, indeed, when the traitor Ragnvald is driven from Norway!" replied Harald. "That will be good news for Thorstein, for an attack in the rear would be fatal. He only has five ships, one of which is mine. His success will depend entirely on his being able to surprise Ragnvald," said Sigurd. Sigurd then told the story of how Thorstein had Christianized the Orkneys and how he had dispatched him immediately on this journey. Thorstein was to remain for three weeks in the islands, baptizing the people. He had arranged to meet Sigurd at Moster, an island on the west coast of Norway, for which Thorstein would direct his course. Sigurd had no opportunity to speak with Freyja until the evening. He was puzzled by her words that morning. Not until Leofric, Sigrid, and he went to her apartments in the evening did he receive an explanation. Freyja told them about Harald's plans for her marriage. "It is a shame!" exclaimed Sigrid. "In England, a girl must yield obedience to her father's wishes, but she is not forced into marrying in this way!" Sigurd was silent, his brows knitted. "I am in a bad position," he said at last. "Of course, the simplest way out would be for you to come on board the "Crane," and for us to join King Thorstein. But I am on a mission here that I cannot neglect. I cannot anger Harald against Thorstein, as such an action would do. Not that I care for my own sake, but it might mean ruin to my king." Leofric agreed with him. "Yes, you must consider your duty to Thorstein. Yet there are two sides to it."

Sigurd shook his head, ending off the discussion. "No," he said firmly. "There are not. At any cost, Harald's finger must be kept out of Thorstein's pie. He's liable to abandon his English trip and turn all his forces against Norway in a sudden fit of rage. That would be fatal to Thorstein at present." "I think I have a plan," Sigrid said, after a pause. "As long as you don't appear in Freyja's escape, it will be all right, won't it?" Sigurd nodded, intrigued. "Well then, give Wulf a few men and that cutter that's on the 'Snake', let them take Freyja on board, and wait for you at some place along the coast. You must leave tomorrow or the next day to rejoin Thorstein, so you can pick them up as you go, and King Harald will think Freyja has fled of her own will." "Good!" cried Sigurd. "What can you say about the plan, Freyja?" "I think it's a good one, too," replied the girl, her dark eyes sparkling. "But all my things are packed up, and I don't want to meet King Thorstein looking like this!" She blushed as a peal of laughter went up from the rest. "Never mind, Freyja," laughed Sigrid. "I will put a chest aboard the 'Crane' tonight. My things will fit you pretty well, and King Thorstein gave me a whole shipload of dresses." "Better put it in the cutter," said Leofric, "for when Harald finds his ward gone, he will search our ships first thing." And so it was arranged, that the next night, Wulf, who had firmly attached himself to the young Haldor, should wait at the dock for Freyja, who insisted on making her way down to the harbor alone.

Chapter 20

THE KING AND THE TOWEL

T he next morning, Wulf was given his instructions. Having grown fond of young Haldor, he and was excited to take on the task. He and Biorn had proven to be wise advisors on many occasions. Later that day, Sigurd and Leofric went hunting with King Harald, and they did not return until well after nightfall. As they arrived at the castle, they saw the courtyard lit up with torches. "What is this? What is all this noise?" King Harald yelled as he quickly dismounted and walked over. Ulf, a gray-haired old seneschal, met him. "My Lord, Lady Freyja of Vendland has vanished without a trace. We have searched the entire castle and town, but there is no sign of her." The King was furious and turned his anger towards Sigurd, accusing him of being a traitor. Sigurd calmly responded that he had been with the King all day and could not have had anything to do with Lady Freyja's disappearance. Harald's anger quickly subsided after Sigurd's response, and he apologized for his behavior. He asked if his men could search the ships, believing Lady Freyja may have fled on one of them seeking refuge with Lady Sigrid. Sigurd and Leofric accepted without hesitation. However, when Sigurd retired for the night, there was still no sign of Lady Freyja. The following morning, Sigurd bid farewell to King Harald, who was preoccupied with Lady Freyja's flight and offered no resistance to his departure. It was an emotional farewell between Sigurd and his young Saxon friends, Leofric and Sigrid. The two of them stood on the deck of the "Crane" until the very end, their eyes filled with tears. Leofric's last words were "Be sure to visit us in England next year. We will look for you in the summer at Lincoln!" Sigurd promised to visit if possible, and the three friends parted ways. As the "Crane" sailed away from the harbor, Sigurd's final glimpse was of Sigrid standing on the forecastle of the "Snake," waving her scarf in farewell. "After we leave this place, where do we find Wulf and Lady Freyja?" Sigurd asked Biorn as they departed.

About twenty miles north was Haldor, and a man was sent with him to guide them to a river mouth where they could lie low without harm. Shortly after noon, Biorn carefully steered the "Crane" towards the land, keeping it near the shore. After thirty minutes, the cutter dashed out as they passed. "Yippee!" shouted Sigurd as Freyja clambered up the side. "Well done, Wulf! King Harald had no clue where his ward had disappeared." "And now, King Thorstein!" Freyja exclaimed gleefully as Wulf carried Sigrid's chest into the cabin and she vanished. However, it was several days before they saw the King because Moster was far up the Norwegian coast. They first saw the high cliffs of Agdir and then sailed alongside the coast heading north. On their journey, they passed Hildirun Bay but did not enter because the location reminded Sigurd of poignant memories. "Have you seen Vidar?" he asked Freyja as they watched the Herey Islands hurry past. "Oh, yes!" she exclaimed. "How could we have forgotten to talk about him earlier! He came to visit me last spring, and just think, Sigurd! He's married!" Sigurd let out a gasp of surprise, and Freyja went on. "Yes, he wedded a girl in Norway and brought her back to Denmark. On his return, he wanted nothing to do with Haldor Sigvald, calling him a coward and a traitor. Haldor is now staying put in Jomsborg. Vidar himself is in the south of Denmark, where his father owned some castles." Sigurd was taken aback to learn that his cousin was married, and he pledged to visit him after Thorstein's mission was accomplished. They reached Moster the following day and before they found the fishing village, they saw Thorstein's four ships, which had arrived a few days ahead. Thorstein was overjoyed to have Freyja back. "It seems you've returned to your friend Oli," he chuckled. "And this time, Oli isn't going to let you leave quickly!" Sigurd told the story of Freyja's escape, and the King praised his Haldor for acting sagely. "If Harald had caught us at this time, Fairhair, it would've been curtains for us. As it stands, you did right by getting the girl away without dispute, and I'm glad that you did."

Thorstein had stopped at Moster for a couple of days, and upon his arrival, he had already laid out a spot on the ground, given Thangbrand an ample amount of resources, and left him there to construct the first-ever church in Norway. Thorstein sailed up north, taking advantage of the wind, following along the coast, but steering clear of the vast number of islands that were scattered near the shoreline. Whenever the wind wasn't in his favor, he would take refuge at the furthest island from the mainland, making sure that Haldor Ragnvald wouldn't hear of his arrival. When evening neared, they finally arrived at Agdaness, located at the entrance of the Firth of Hlidskjalf. When the ship was anchored, and the awnings put up, King Thorstein paid a visit to the "Crane." "Now, Sigurd," the King said, "I'm seeking your advice. Thorir Klakke is aboard my ship, and as you know, my brothers had exposed his plans when he tried to bribe them. Well, Haldor Ragnvald's men are lurking in the nearby forest, awaiting our arrival. Thorir is going to take me to the shore, pretending to have a plan of action, and that's where I might be killed. I'd like to hear your take on this." After pondering for a while, Sigurd responded, "It seems to me, Thorstein, that it would be suitable for the traitor to fall into his own trap. Tonight, let's send twenty of our men to the shore to hide, and when Ragnvald's men appear, let our men charge them and drive them out. Afterward, we'll execute Thorir." "That's an excellent plan," the King replied. "I don't desire to take a person's life, but culprits like this need to be punished, and death is the most fitting penalty for treason. So be it." The next morning, Sigurd, who was watching from the "Crane," saw Thorir and the King walking alone to the shore. They strolled along the coastline, and then Thorir signaled with his glove. In a matter of moments, a group of men emerged from the woods. However, more men arose from the nearby boulders along the shore, causing the first group to flee. Two of the fleeing men fell upon Thorir as the King watched on, and the disloyal man met his demise. After that, Thorstein walked down to the water and called out to Sigurd to come ashore, which the young Haldor promptly did.

"Fairhair," Thorstein called out, "let us go and seek news of Haldor Ragnvald. We must catch up to him soon if he is in Hlidskjalf before these men spread word of our arrival." They climbed up the hill, leaving their men behind, and soon stumbled upon a quaint farmhouse. Behind the house was a small pasture where a few cows lazily grazed. As they neared the door, an old woman appeared inside. "Good day, kind dame," Thorstein greeted her. "Might we trouble you for a drink of fresh milk? We are travelers and will gladly pay for what we take."

"Of course, my friends!" the woman replied warmly. "Come in and I will fetch some for you." While the woman was out of sight, Thorstein and Sigurd washed their hands at the well. Once inside, the King dried his hands with a nearby towel when the woman returned and snatched it from his grasp. "You must not have been brought up with manners," she scolded. "Do you not know to use only what you need?" Thorstein replied calmly, "I suppose I shall rise so high that I can dry my hands in the middle of the towel." Sigurd could not hold back his laughter, causing the woman to glare at him. After finishing their milk and paying the woman, Thorstein asked, "Do you happen to know where Haldor Ragnvald is?" "Last night, my son told me he was in hiding," replied the woman. "In hiding?" Thorstein was taken aback. "Why is that?" "Where have you been?" she asked incredulously. "Ragnvald has become so cruel and tyrannical lately that no one can bear his rule. Just two days ago, the bonders rose up against him under Orm Lugg because of his outrageous demands in Gauladale. They separated him from his ships and forced him into the forest, and no one knows where he went. My son said that they were going to search for him at Thora of Rimul's abode, as she is a relative of the Jarls." Thorstein and Sigurd exchanged knowing looks. They had their next destination.

"Oh, my, my!" exclaimed the King, rushing back to the ships. "Do you not believe that the heavens are on my side, Fairhair? I arrive in Norway just when Ragnvald has pushed the peasants to rebel. He is now cut off from his troops and vessels, lurking in the woods, and most likely dead by now! Hurry, let us cross the Firth and make our way to Gauladale!" With swift urgency, they relayed the news to the other ships and set sail towards Gauladale, steering their ships briskly across the Firth of Hlidskjalf.

Chapter 21

THE DEATH OF RAGNVALD

A s they left the safety of the bay and made their way across the narrow passage of the Firth, Thorstein and his men spotted three ships sailing on the opposite shore. Thorstein knew without a doubt that these were Ragnvald's ships. As the fleets drew closer, the three ships suddenly turned towards the shore, mistaking Thorstein's ships for enemies. Without hesitation, Thorstein charged forward, pursuing the three ships until they reached a sandbar. The frightened crew members jumped off the ships, swimming towards the shore, but one man caught Thorstein's attention. He was a large and handsome man, swimming in front of Thorstein's ship. The King shouted at him to stop, but he wouldn't listen. In anger, Thorstein grabbed the tiller and flung it at the man. The heavy object struck him on the head, and he disappeared beneath the water. Thorstein's men jumped off their ship and started chasing the flying men, killing some and capturing others. The captives revealed that the man whom Thorstein had killed was Erland, the son of Haldor Ragnvald. Furthermore, they informed the king that they were heading towards Haldor's aid. The prisoners also disclosed that Haldor's forces were in disarray, that the bonders had revolted throughout the whole district, and that nobody knew where Haldor was hiding. King Thorstein landed some of his men ashore and gave them instructions to announce who he was, why he had come, and to ask all the bonders to meet him in Gauladale the following day. The fleet then steered east, going up the Firth. That very afternoon, the King arrived safely on the shore of Gauladale. Upon landing, Thorstein found a massive gathering of the chief bonders and leaders of the revolt against Ragnvald in progress. Soon after they learned of his presence, they welcomed him warmly, shedding tears of joy. Thorstein introduced his chiefs, which included Sigurd, his trusted and reliable advisor. The assembly then settled down, and one of the older leaders of the peasants rose to speak to the King.

The news of the attack on Ragnvald had spread like wildfire, and the young Haldor Eirik was sure to retaliate with brutal force. But the bonders were resolute: Haldor Ragnvald must die. His deeds were deemed unforgivable, and justice must be served. At the assembly, King Thorstein was called upon to lead them. The men of Thorstein welcomed the news with great joy. Thorstein traced his lineage all the way back to the time of Harald Fairhair, and his noble blood was a beacon of hope to the bonders. They set out that evening with purpose, journeying towards Rimul where they believed Haldor Ragnvald was hiding. En route, they found a cloak, belonging to the man they were hunting. The discovery of his horse's lifeless body only strengthened the belief that Haldor Ragnvald had perished in the river. But the old bonder's words rang true to Sigurd, and others soon agreed. They could not let their guard down. With a newfound conviction, they pushed on, arriving at Rimul where Lady Thora lived. They thoroughly searched the homestead but to no avail. Thorstein stood on a large stone near the barn, his voice ringing out loud and clear. "Men, we have done our best to find Haldor Ragnvald but our efforts have been unsuccessful. At this time we can do no more. But know, that I will reward whoever shall slay the Haldor and bring me his head with a fitting gift and payment. The bonders left Rimul and took temporary quarters at Ladi, a large farm and village belonging to the Kings of Norway. It was there that they waited, ready for the next move. The air was thick with anticipation, and the bonders knew that they had to be vigilant. For the fate of their land hung in the balance, and the heavy responsibility now rested on the shoulders of King Thorstein.

The sun had barely risen when the men were brought ashore from the ships. The bonders, or local farmers, were summoned and word was spread throughout the land that King Thorstein, son of King Triggve, had come to take control from Ragnvald. A General Assembly of the People was called to convene immediately at Hlidskjalf, the seat of power. But the day's events weren't yet over. The very next afternoon, King Thorstein was approached by a curious man outside a farmhouse in Ladi. The man was wearing the collar of a slave and carried a large package under his arm. "What do you want?" asked King Thorstein. As a response, the man opened his package and displayed a human head. Sigurd couldn't bear to look at it, but they all knew whose head it was:

it belonged to Haldor Ragnvald of Norway. Without delay, Thorstein ordered his men to take the slave into custody and demanded an explanation. The man was a tooth-thrall, a slave given to Ragnvald when he cut his first teeth. After fleeing with Ragnvald from the bonders, they sought refuge in a cave beneath the pigsty on Lady Thora's land. It was the same yard where Thorstein had offered a reward for Ragnvald's head. "Why did you betray your master?" asked Thorstein angrily. "Your promise of a reward, King," replied the slave. "Your voice carried clearly, and I knew what was expected of me. So, I killed him in his sleep and brought his head to you." Hearing this, Thorstein's eyes filled with rage. "Seize him, men!" he bellowed. "I made a promise that I intend to keep. This will teach all those who come after us not to betray their lords. You were wicked, but he was your master and a good one to you. You were bound to him by sacred oaths, and for that, your reward is to be fitting indeed. Take him out and behead him!" When the deed was done, Thorstein took the slave's head, along with Ragnvald's, on his ship and sailed to Nidarholm, an island used for executing criminals. The two heads were mounted on the gallows for all to see. That evening, King Thorstein sat with his leaders in the farmhouse at Ladi, content in knowing that he had dealt with his enemies accordingly.

"My friends," declared Thorstein in a serious tone, "Haldor Ragnvald has met his fate, and I doubt Haldor Eirik will have the courage to challenge us. Soon, the General Assembly will convene, and I believe that the people will choose me to be their king. It is my belief that only through the assistance of God was Ragnvald so easily defeated. Additionally, the time has come for Norway to abandon idolatry and pagan beliefs in order to accept the Holy Truth." "You have come with me from Ireland," Thorstein reminded his companions, "and I implore you to consider giving your lives, if need be, to spread the Word of God." "Aye!" cheered the crowd, and following a council, they decided that their first action would be to eradicate the worship of Thor and Odin in the grand temple in Hlidskjalf. Sigurd reminisced about his experience with Vidar in that temple, and the thought of replacing Thor's golden statue with the Cross filled him with exhilaration. The King's words had stirred a fire within the hearts of everyone present, and Bishop Sigurd spoke passionately in support of Thorstein's intentions. For the next few weeks, they remained at Ladi, with Freyja settling into the large farmhouse. There was little to do except sit tight until the bonders gathered for the General Assembly. For this reason, Thorstein delayed the dismantling of the great temple to Odin in Ladi. It was unwise to anger the bonders before he had been elected. Regardless, he was confident of election. Most of the powerful individuals in the region had come to Ladi and met with him. His attractive physique and regal bearing had left a strong impression, and his reputation as a noteworthy warrior did not hurt his chances. Eventually, word arrived that delegates from all eight areas of Norway had convened at Hlidskjalf, at the mouth of the Firth. Thorstein and his troops set off in that direction. With his previous interactions with key figures around the country, he believed that his election as king was almost a certainty. Thorstein was known for his chivalrous figure, and his status as one of the top warriors of his generation only sealed the deal.

The party, including Thorstein, Sigurd, and Freyja, arrived at Hlidskjalf and were given luxurious accommodations in the palace of Haldor Ragnvald. Two days later, they made their way to the Assembly where a massive crowd had gathered from the entire Hlidskjalf district. Once the Assembly had been established, King Thorstein rose to his feet. His red-gold hair whipped in the wind, the sun casting a golden sheen on his armor and scarlet cloak. "I have offered myself to be King over you," Thorstein proclaimed. "You must expect the wrath of Haldor Eirik for the attack on his father, unless you acquire protection. On the other hand, I am tasked with the challenge of regaining my father's kingdom after being absent for so long." Thorstein proceeded to provide a brief account of his life and adventures, starting from his childhood up until his discovery of Thorir Klakke's deceit. He spoke of his journey to Norway and the death of Ragnvald, concluding with a bold statement. "I believe there is no man in Norway with more legal right and descent than I to the crown. But I need to be made King by you, the Assembly of the People. If you do so, I will protect you and govern you in accordance with Norway's ancient laws." The tale of

Thorstein's exile and suffering moved the people deeply, and they were already leaning in his favor. As he took his seat, half of the delegates rose to their feet. "Skoal! Thorstein Triggveson, skoal! We want you to be our King and nobody else! Skoal!" Blaring horns mixed with cheers as Sigurd flapped his ensign in the breeze. A quick silence followed the sight of the Cross, but it was brief. The people quickly resumed their shouts, which reverberated through the bay and the town and echoed back from the hills. "Skoal to King Thorstein! Skoal!"

Chapter 22

THE SACRIFICE TO THOR

A nd so it was that Thorstein Triggveson, proclaimed King over all of Norway, took the reins of the land in accordance with ancient laws. The officers of the people ceded the rule to him while the bonder people swore an oath of fidelity, promising to support him in his quest to conquer the entire kingdom and defend it against invaders. Thorstein, for his part, pledged to respect the laws and the rights of the people. As the day wore on, Sigurd and Freyja, witnesses to the coronation, returned to the hall, but Thorstein was nowhere to be seen. For days, he was busy garnering the support of various leaders who had rallied to his cause, gathering men and dispatching messengers throughout Norway to spread the news of his election. Soon after, word reached them that the levies were no longer required. Haldor Eirik and Harald, his brother, had already fled to Sweden upon hearing of their father's passing. With the whole country now under Thorstein's reign, the people welcomed the return of the royal line of rulers with open arms, bidding farewell to the ousted Ragnvald, who was now known as "Ragnvald the Bad." Despite his eagerness to spread the gospel among his people, Thorstein's namesake, the Bishop and other leaders warned him that he must solidify his hold on the country first, for they foresaw that his intention to overturn the old faith would trigger chaos and uprisings. Nevertheless, the King relented somewhat, refusing to inhabit Hlidskjalf, where the great temple of Thor was located, and instead establishing a separate town, Nidaros, just a few miles away. And so the fall and early winter slipped by. However, rumors soon began to surface that Thorstein was not a follower of the old gods, and serious disruptions erupted throughout the land. The bonders grew increasingly disenchanted with the new King's unorthodox beliefs, distancing themselves from him. Then, one day, reports surfaced that numerous gatherings of bonders had been held at massive temples, with solemn sacrifices to the old gods. There, they vowed that they would not permit Thorstein to bring the "White Christ" to Norway.

All saw that action was necessary to protect the kingdom. The heart of the land was in the Hlidskjalf area, where the population was densest and where the capital was. Thorstein knew that if he could establish Christianity here, the rest of Norway would likely follow suit. Thus, he called for another General Assembly at Frosta, near the capital. However, on the way, the bonders intercepted his messengers and replaced the call for the meeting with a war arrow. At the assembly, he found himself surrounded by a huge host of armed, angry chiefs. Thorstein, accompanied only by Sigurd and a few men, knew he was trapped. But he endeavored to placate the assembly on the first day. When he mentioned Christianity, several leaders objected and forbade him from speaking about religion that day. Sigurd, sensing the hostility in the air, conferred with Thorstein in their tent that night. "I have a plan," he said, "that might save us from further trouble." "What is it?" exclaimed Thorstein. "I'm at my wit's end." Sigurd shared his plan at length that night. The next morning, Thorstein stood before the assembly and gave a brief speech. "Let us honor the compact we made before," he said, "to strengthen and support each other. To that end, I will attend your great sacrifice two weeks from now at the temple in Hlidskjalf. Afterward, we will consult on the faith we will hold and agree to stay with our chosen faith." The bonders cheered, thinking that Thorstein was conceding. Thus, the other matters for which the assembly had been convened passed peacefully. When Thorstein returned to Nidaros, a town he founded, several men from Iceland were baptized shortly after Yuletide. Many traders and others who remained through the winter at Thorstein's court also received baptism.

For two weeks straight, Sigurd and the King worked tirelessly to perfect their plan. The bonders' primary opponent of Christianity was a fierce chief named Ironbeard, who also acted as the priest at Moeri, a nearby town located near Hlidskjalf. Their plan was to destroy all forms of resistance to Christianity in the district at the winter sacrifice, taking place in the great temple in Moeri. Invitations were sent to all chiefs of the bonders, for a feast that would occur at Nidaros three days before the winter sacrifice. Sigurd extended invitations to the most influential leaders from the Hlidskjalf districts, and all had accepted, except for Ironbeard and a few others. On the scheduled morning, the invited chiefs flocked into town, on foot, horseback, and skis. Many voyaged over the ice from across the bay. By the following morning, the new city was swarming with men, each chief bringing a troop with him. Early in the morning, Thorstein and his court attended a church service at the new church, with all of the visitors refusing to witness the event. Immediately after, Sigurd led a group of fifty men to the harbor. There, they wore skates, and a young chap named Haldor led them to Ladi, which was only a mere three miles away across the ice, though more on foot. After taking off their skates, Sigurd and his troops traveled from the shore up to the temple on a hill. Nudging his axe, Sigurd struck the door. Within five minutes, the entrance broke down while the few priests who resided nearby watched on hopelessly. Sigurd and his men collected all of the idols, created a display out of them, and set them on fire. It was a demonstration to show the beholding priests and bonders that their gods lacked strength. Following this, the valuables inside the temple were removed, and the temple itself was set ablaze. Once done, Sigurd and his men then formed a cross out of a pair of wooden beams and erected it in the snow atop the ruins of the idols. Then, as the bonders quickly gathered in large numbers, Sigurd strode forth to speak: "Companions, we are present by order of the King. Today you have all witnessed the powerlessness of your gods compared to the real God. Your leaders are presently in Nidaros but they will return as Christian men and not heathens anymore."

Sigurd and his band of warriors sailed back into Nidaros, their boat weighed down with the plunder they had taken from the temple. As they approached the harbor mouth, a man appeared before them, announcing that the King had called an urgent Assembly and that they must hurry to the palace. Without delay, Sigurd raced to the palace, instructing his men to wait outside until he signaled them with his horn. Once inside, he joined the scores of great leaders gathered there just as the Assembly was beginning. King Thorstein stood at the head of the room, his gaze stern as he addressed the assembled chiefs and bonders. He reminded them that they had chosen him to be their king and had given him the realm of Norway. However, he also recounted how, at a recent General Assembly, many of them had refused to hear him preach the gospel of Christ, forcing him to appease them with promises of attending the winter sacrifice. "I have shamed false gods throughout the land, burning their temples and images to make way for the Cross of the true God," Thorstein said. "But I cannot ignore the oath I made to you all at that Assembly. And so, I propose to offer the greatest sacrifice of all: human life." The room buzzed with excitement at the thought of such a momentous offering, but their joy was short-lived. Thorstein went on to say that he did not believe slaves or criminals should be offered to the gods. Instead, he suggested that the gods would be appeased by the blood of noble men: great chiefs and powerful bonders. "Since you have refused to release me from my oath," Thorstein continued, "I must proceed with the sacrifice. We must do our best to appease the gods so that they may favor us. Am I right?" A doubtful murmuring arose from the gathered men, unsure of what the King meant. They looked to Thorstein, handsome and unyielding, waiting for him to clarify his intentions.

"So," he began, his voice echoing across the great hall, "I shall make a sacrifice of such magnitude that it will go down in history as the greatest ever made to appease the gods. You must be eager for their favor and blessings, and so I have chosen you, Orm Lugg, Asbiorn of Orness, Stirkar of Gimsa, and Kar of Gryting, to be offered on the high altar of Thor at Thrandeim. And once this has been accomplished, I will then choose six other men, the most honorable and esteemed in this district, to be sacrificed as well. For it is through these sacrifices that the gods will send us bountiful harvests and everlasting peace."

Chapter 23

HOW THE CHIEFS WERE BAPTIZED

The chiefs gazed at the King in disbelief as he stood there, smirking at his own words. But as the meaning of his ironic speech dawned on them, they sprang to their feet with fury, screaming in protest. Thorstein raised his hand to quiet the uproar. "Wait a moment! You don't seem to be so keen on the company of your gods. Are you beginning to doubt their power to save you? If that's the case, and you want me to release myself from my oath, I'll be happy to have you all baptized and embrace the mighty, gentle, and kind God that I and my men serve." At these words, Sigurd blew his horn, and the doors of the hall flew open. Thorstein's men came in carrying the spoils from the Ladi temple, placing them at their feet, while other armed men silently took positions around the hall. "Here," Thorstein said rudely, pointing to the temple utensils and trappings. "You can see how powerless your gods are to save even their own possessions! So think it over. I'll be back in a few minutes." Thorstein strode out of the hall, followed by Sigurd. He was about to express his joy to the boy when they heard an angry voice. "What's this story I hear, King Thorstein?" Startled, they saw the old English bishop Sigurd in his vestments, his face stern and cold as Thorstein bowed to him. "Is this true? That you're holding the Hlidskjalf chiefs in the great hall, forcing them to choose between baptism and death? Answer me!" Astounded, Thorstein stared at the Bishop, then after a moment, his eyes fell. "Well, Bishop, it's true, certainly. What do you mean?" The old man's eyes flared. "Do you think this is the way to spread the gospel of Christ? Is baptism a thing to be imposed on people, or are they expected to choose it willingly? Thorstein Triggveson, it would be better to lose your kingdom and flee back over the ocean than to do this!" The boy spoke up. "Bishop, it's my fault; I suggested the idea. But why is it so terrible? After all, didn't these same chiefs trap Thorstein only a few weeks ago?"

Bishop Sigurd glared at Thorstein. "What does it matter to you? Do what you will with the corpses, Thorstein, but do not force their spirits! Let them come to Christ willingly." His tone softened. "I understand that your fervor has gotten the best of you, but King and Haldor, this is not Christianity. Christ said, 'Come unto me.' Do you believe he would have men beaten and threatened by swords, who died to save men?" Thorstein bowed his head, and Sigurd fell to his knees. "Forgive me, Bishop! I had not considered it from that perspective; now I see how wrong it was!" The Bishop placed his hand on Sigurd's head. "And what about you, Thorstein? Do you not see I am right? Do you still need to be led by this boy?" Fixing his piercing gaze on the elder, Thorstein slowly nodded. "I see, Bishop, and I will follow your unspoken wishes." He turned gradually, and Sigurd followed him to the great hall's entrance. The room fell silent as they entered, and Thorstein ordered his men to leave the building, standing silently as they filed out. Then, climbing onto the throne, he spoke bitterly: "Chieftains, I arrived preaching the Word of God, the gospel of peace and salvation, but my deeds have been those of a pagan, and worse. It is no wonder you refused to accept my faith! I now see that I have wronged you; I am ready to make amends and lead as a true Christian. Go in peace; those who wish to embrace Christianity will be welcomed. If you desire to have a heathen King rule over you, I will return to where I came from, without wielding fire and sword in the land." The chiefs gawked at the King, and Orm Lugg, one of the greatest, spoke up: "Is this true, King? Are we free to return home?" "Yes," replied Thorstein, with a flush on his face. "I have shown myself to be a poor Christian, my friends, but forgive me for now. Go, and I will abide by whatever you want." One by one, in silence and astonishment, the chieftains left the hall, and only Sigurd remained with the King. The youth then grasped Thorstein's hand, tears streaming down his face: "Thorstein, we were mistaken, but how you must suffer! Will you go back to Ireland if the chiefs refuse to embrace the gospel?"

"Yes, my friend," Thorstein's voice was soft and low, "the Bishop has shown me something that I cannot fully express. My pride has been shattered. The Hammer of Thor is not the same as Christ's Cross. I believed that the Cross could be used as a weapon, like Thor's Hammer, but I was wrong. The Cross represents gentle humility and pity. Yes, my-" The doors suddenly burst open, and the chiefs entered to the King's amazement. Their faces had changed, and their resistance had given way to a new emotion. "King Thorstein," Orm spoke as the representative of the chiefs, "we have found the palace unguarded and the streets clear, just as you said. We have resisted your faith not because we love the old gods, but because we saw no difference in the White Christ. You preached one thing but did the opposite. But today, you have shown us something new. We have found in you a man who is strong, proud, and used to ruling the wills of others. We have rejoiced in you as our King. Today, we have learned that there is something stronger than pride and will, something that can overcome all of it, and because of this, we accept the Cross of Christ from your hand willingly." Thorstein looked at the men around him with tears streaming down his face, unable to speak. He took each of their hands and said, "My friends, this is a victory where I had found a defeat. I cannot express what this means to me, but I know that we will never forget this day. Haldor Sigurd and I have learned a lesson from you and from ourselves. May God grant that we never have to learn it again!"

Sigurd called for the Bishop and recounted the events of their journey. Without delay, the chiefs and their entourages were baptized in the brand-new church erected by Thorstein. Later that night, Thorstein and Sigurd sat together in a room, discussing the day's happenings until the wee hours. Thorstein, the king, had given Freyja, Sigurd's love interest, a portion of Haldor Ragnvald's seized property to replace the ones she had in Vendland so that she could live like a dignitary. Additionally, he declared himself her guardian but joked that he might force her to marry if he had to. Thorstein promised Sigurd an earldom once he had put the country in order. That same night, Freyja asked Thorstein about his plans. He shook his head, pondering the gravity of the events of their baptism day. All the major chiefs from the Hlidskjalf districts were baptized that day, and Thorstein felt the bond established would be unbreakable. Everyone but Ironbeard, that is. Thorstein intended to persuade Ironbeard during the winter sacrifice to join them as a baptized member. The next day, they burned down the old temple of the war god without any resistance, and many of the newly baptized chiefs pledged their loyalty to Thorstein, willingly or by sending soldiers. The idols were brought out and burned before the people to signify the destruction of their gods. Sigurd wished that Vidar could be with them, recalling their escapade with Haldor Ragnvald, but he was too far south. By noon, they had completed their task and made their way back to Nidaros. The bonders' threats against Thorstein had diminished, and many of them flocked to Nidaros to be baptized by the Bishop since their greatest chiefs had already converted.

The day after the temple of Hlidskjalf was destroyed, Thorstein and his men set sail for Moeri, where the winter sacrifice was held. They braved the waters of Hlidskjalf Firth on their largest ships until they arrived at Moeri on the day of the sacrifice. The King demanded that the people hold an Assembly first and sent Sigurd ashore to make the request. To Fairhair's surprise, a great multitude of people from all over the countryside had gathered, including Ironbeard and his men. They all agreed to Thorstein's demand, and the Assembly was held on the plain before the temple. When the commotion and chatter died down, Thorstein took his seat and rose to address the bonders. He revealed what had transpired in his hall at Nidaros, admitting his mistake and that he no longer wished to force a religion upon them that they did not want. Sigurd noticed a shift in the demeanor of the bonders before him. They exchanged glances and began whispering amongst themselves. Suddenly, Ironbeard stood up from his seat. He was an immense man, towering over the rest, with a beard as gray as iron that swept over his chest. Wearing the robes of a priest of Thor, he lifted his hand and began to speak, his words resonating with great dignity and authority.

Chapter 24

THORSTEIN'S ATONEMENT

The priest's voice boomed through the temple, "King Thorstein, we cannot allow you to disrespect our religion. It is our wish that you make the same sacrifices as Haldor Ragnvaldas and the other kings before you did. When King Ragnvald, the foster son of King Athelstan of England, wanted to convert to Christianity, the bonders were too strong for him, and he yielded to the old ways. You are to follow his example, for our minds have not changed since the Assembly where you promised to visit this temple." Ironbeard sat down, and the bonders applauded him loudly. Thorstein was angry at the chief's demands, but he controlled his temper and rose to speak. "My friends, I promised to visit your temple, and I will do so now, before the sacrifices. The Assembly is closed." Thorstein motioned for Sigurd and the other men to join him. After disarming themselves, they walked towards the temple. Thorstein held a gold-mounted staff of heavy wood in his hand and whispered to Sigurd, "Haldor, do as I do, and act fast." As they entered the temple, they saw many images surrounding them. The largest idol, adorned with silver and gold, stood in a position of honor. Thorstein's men filled the temple while the bonders watched from the doorway. Without a sound, King Thorstein walked up to the giant idol and, raising his staff, struck it. The idol fell to the stone floor and broke into two parts. At the same time, Sigurd and the other men rushed to the remaining images, sweeping them from their pedestals. A horror-stricken cry erupted from the bonders, and Ironbeard picked up a spear and poised it, preparing to throw it at the King. One of Thorstein's men fired an arrow and shot Ironbeard in the chest, causing him to fall to the temple's threshold. The bonders retreated in terror and King Thorstein turned to the man who fired the arrow. "Who shot that arrow?" he shouted. "I did, King Thorstein," the man replied. "I did it to save your life. Ironbeard had a spear pointed at you. Look, it's still in his hand!"

Thorstein gazed down at the fallen leader, recognizing the truth in his words. He turned to Sigurd, issuing a command. "Order the Assembly called. Tell them not to be afraid." As the people took their places once more, Thorstein emerged from the temple. Standing on the steps he said, "Friends and bonders, I came not to spill blood. The death of Ironbeard was a tragedy, and I regret that he sealed his own fate. As I stated earlier, I will not force anyone to abandon their beliefs. I have seen the error in that path. Nonetheless, a handful of days prior, other leaders, some who stand before you, accepted the Cross of Christ from me. Now, I offer this same opportunity to all of you." Thorstein paused, allowing his message to sink in. "You have all witnessed the fall of your gods; they lay shattered and powerless. Where is their might now? The true God has safeguarded my life, bringing me to this land and granting me this kingdom. Whether you choose to accept it or not, His teachings will reign supreme in Norway before long." A bonder rose, offering his rebuttal. "Your words are kind, King, and carry the air of truth and fairness. It is clear to us that the gods have perished, unable to stand against the Cross of Christ. That being said, the slaying of Ironbeard was an ill deed, regardless of its intended outcome. Before we proceed, we must ask if you intend to punish his murderer." The bonder descended back into his seat, everyone's gaze was trained on Thorstein, waiting for his response. The King sat silently for a moment, struggling with his decision. Finally, his expression cleared. "I will not punish the man, for he saved my life. However, hold your tongues for a moment, for I have more to say. Is there anyone present who is related to Ironbeard?" Two men stood, acknowledging the question. "We are distant kin, Your Highness. Yet, besides his daughter, we are his only mourners."

King Thorstein removed his helmet and gathered the attention of his people. "Dear people, this is a just gathering, with the authority to pass judgment and punish criminals, including the power to impose penalties. I appoint you two farmers as judges, and I take responsibility for the death of Ironbeard. Whatever is the verdict, I will abide by it in exchange for his death. If you demand my life, or exile, or a significant fine, I will grant it, and my men will not threaten you with punishment." Silence gripped the people, and Sigurd looked at Thorstein with admiration and amazed. Bishop Sigurd had not preached in vain! A quiet acknowledgment of Thorstein's gesture swept through the crowd. After a moment's contemplation, the two kinsmen of Ironbeard stood up.

"King Thorstein, your words have humiliated us, who showed up with weapons
and the intent to engage in war. It's a new chapter in Norway's history where
Kings submit themselves to the law like lay persons, and it seems fair to us that
you do so. The law says that for taking a life, the relatives of the deceased can
claim the life of the killer, or demand payment in land and possessions. Faere
Ironbeard, the sole daughter of the deceased, is affluent and from a respectable
family. As her family, we have decided that you offer her your hand in marriage
and bestow upon her land befitting a queen." King Thorstein's men growled
in disagreement, even Sigurd appeared flabbergasted. King Thorstein had been
thinking of marrying one of the daughters of the Swedish King to solidify their
countries' bond. However, Thorstein calmed the protests with a hand gesture
and addressed the farmers.

Friends, hear my words and let them be known as true. I agree to this lawful
judgment, and do so with a spirit of goodwill. I entrust the responsibility to
you, my two men, to ensure that the maid is safely transported to Nidaros
before Eastertide, so that I may marry her and make her the Queen of this land.
It is the least I can do, I believe, after my men killed her father and left her
destitute. If this course of action does not meet with her approval, I entrust
you to choose another measure of punishment for me to fulfill, and I will do
most faithfully. This pledge I make on the Cross. Thorstein took his seat in the
midst of an uproarious approval from the bonders, and a group of men rose
and insisted on speaking. One of them was selected to speak on their behalf,
and he addressed the King, saying: "My lord, when I departed from my home,
it was my firm intention to resist your faith to the last drop of my blood. But
now I am proud to accept baptism at your hand, and to pledge my loyalty to
you once more." Thorstein was taken aback, and one by one the other bonders
rose and made the same declaration of loyalty. Then Thorstein sent for Bishop
Sigurd, who had remained behind at the ships for fear of an attack by Ironbeard,
and turned to address the bonders. "My loyal countrymen, nothing could bring
me greater joy than this. It is my deepest desire that Norway should become a
Christian land. Once all the leaders of Hlidskjalf and the surrounding districts

have received baptism, we will encounter little opposition from the rest of the kingdom. To demonstrate the earnestness of your commitment, I ask that you finish the destruction of this temple to the old gods, and on its ruins, I will erect a church to the one true God at my own expense." The bonders erupted in a deafening roar, brandishing their weapons. Without hesitation, they hurried towards the temple, carrying out the shattered images and heaving them into the snow. Others stripped the temple of its embellishments and set it ablaze. As the pile of idols was consumed by the flames, Bishop Sigurd arrived, fresh from the ships.

He heard the tale on the journey up the hill, and as the King approached, he clasped Thorstein's hand firmly, without speaking. They began the work of conversion right away, with Sigurd and the rest of the King's men acting as godfathers to the new Christians who had been born again. After this was done, the afternoon waned. They made arrangements with the leaders of the community to build a church, bury Ironbeard, and send his daughter Gudrun to Nidaros for Easter. When all of this was done, Thorstein's warriors embarked, and the King sailed down the Firth towards Nidaros. A few days earlier, the Firth had opened up, even though it was still wintertime. The temperature had increased slightly, and a channel had been dug from above Moeri to the sea. When they arrived in the harbor that evening, they found the town lit by torches, and several newly arrived ships, or rather, small cutters, in the harbor. "I'm curious what this means," the King said as they approached the anchorage. "When we left the city yesterday, I hadn't heard anything about visitors, and it's strange that the town is all lit up!" So, before the ships could anchor, Thorstein and Sigurd jumped into a small boat and were rowed ashore. Great fires had been lit on either side of the harbor, making everything visible, and a group of men greeted them as they disembarked. "What's all this commotion about?" the King asked, looking perplexed. A jumbled clamor responded to him. "One at a time!" Thorstein shouted, and one of the men stepped forward. "My lord King, we were driven out of our homes and come from the north. There, two chiefs, Raud the Strong and Thori Hart, have revolted against the Christ. They've gathered a fleet and are approaching you. They intend to rebuild the temples of Thor and Odin while burning down the churches you've built. We Christians barely escaped with our lives, fleeing on our small boats. In a few days, the heathens will enter the Firth unless you stop them first!"

Chapter 25

THE WRESTLING MATCH

T horstein rushed to the great hall where the fugitives were waiting to tell their story. The two Northern chieftains had taken advantage of the rare, warm weather to sail a fleet down the coast in hopes of catching the King off guard, just as he had caught Haldar Ragnvald. After a quick consultation with his Bishop, Sigurd, and other leaders, Thorstein knew the King had to act fast. If they embanked and sailed out of the Firth that night, they could reach the entrance by morning and wait for the heathen fleet there. The King agreed, and word was sent to his men to return to their ships. But the Hlidskjalf chiefs refused to go home, insisting that they and their men would be of use if it came to a battle. With several hundred warriors backing them, the King was overjoyed and set up their standards on his ships. A few hours later, Thorstein and Sigurd left Nidaros with a dozen ships while the rest were taken off of their winter dry docks. As they rowed down the Firth all night, Thorstein and Sigurd tried to rest as much as they could. The day had been terribly hard on both of them, and they needed every bit of energy for the battle to come. The week of warm weather felt like a gift from heaven, and many of the men saw it as a sign of Thorstein's favor. Although no one expected the warm weather to last, few of the oldest men could remember a winter when Hlidskjalf Firth had opened before April which is a hopeful sign for the King's impending battle.

By morning, the Norsemen had left the cape of Agdaness, the very same spot where the treacherous Thorkel had met his just fate. The group, led by the King himself, stopped at this location and ordered the ships to heave to, awaiting the arrival of six other ships scheduled to join them from Nidaros. All day passed, yet there was no sign of the rebels. A few small ships carrying additional fugitives came down the coast offering Thorstein news that the notorious Raud and Thori were now only within fifteen miles to the north. The pair had landed at Theksdale and were trying to gather as many men as they could muster from across the land, hoping to bolster their forces in the rebellion. That afternoon, the reinforcements arrived as scheduled from Nidaros, prompting the King to convene a council of sorts upon his ship, the "Crane." Mindful of keeping bloodshed to a minimum, the King asked for suggestions from his men on how they could win the rebels over. Sigurd had an idea that he felt was worth sharing. He explained to the King and the others that his forecastle man, old Biorn, had a theory. Biorn predicted that a heavy frost would set in tonight, considering that all of this warm weather was highly unusual. Biorn maintained that if a frost did in fact return tonight, it would be no light one, thus blocking off the Firth. Sigurd shared his observation that any ships lying along the shore would be frozen quickly, especially if they were located in a tight bay location like Theksdale. He suggested that Raud and Thori might not pay enough attention to their ships, perhaps carelessly drawing them ashore or anchoring them nearby. He believed that if they seized the opportunity and attacked them suddenly, their enemies would likely be so devastated from the loss of their ships and far from home without means of retreat that they would ultimately surrender. The King and his cohorts were ecstatic about Sigurd's idea, considering it to be the perfect solution. However, they were also mindful of the fact that this plan was highly contingent on whether or not a frost set in. Regardless of the weather, they had already decided that they would leave the land, avoiding the possibility of their own ships getting frozen in place.

The chiefs went back to their ships, each to their own, and set sail. They sailed out two or three miles to sea, where they lay quiet in the tossing waters. At sunset, Bishop Sigurd, who was on board the "Crane," conducted a solemn service. He made a prayer to God to favor their enterprise, and all the men on the ships joined in the responses. Sigurd Fairhair was moved by the sight. Eighteen ships, all filled with men, with many who had just recently stopped worshiping idols, were gathered together in the sunset glow, praying devoutly to Jesus Christ. As soon as the sun set, darkness fell on the ocean, bringing with it bitter cold. Many of the men had not expected this, and had left their furs and cloaks behind. So, the others divided theirs among all. Some of the ships had bales of merchandise on them, and at the king's command, these were opened by torchlight, and given to those without cloaks. Midnight came, and it was clear that the intense cold would close the Firth, as Sigurd had predicted, leaving the enemy helpless. The men shouted with joy, and the ships were turned north, swiftly rowing toward Theksdale. There was not even the slightest breath of wind, and the cold grew more intense with every passing minute. At sunrise, the pilots announced that they were not far from their destination. One hour later, they rounded the islands outside Theksdale Bay. However, there was a line of ragged ice nearly a foot thick that formed during the night and blocked their path. In a hurry, but without mishap, the crews disembarked and made their way across the headland, guided by those who knew the coast. They left men on board the ships to keep them safe. Before them, they saw the army of revolt and their fleet, held fast in the bonds of ice along the shore. "Come," exclaimed Thorstein to his nearest leaders, "we must lose no time, for they are cutting the ships out of the ice!"

He was a formidable presence, with broad shoulders and fierce eyes that glared at Thorstein with hostility. Thori Hart trailed behind him, more reserved in his movements but no less imposing. They stood before the King and his men, weapons at their sides, ready for whatever would come next. "Have we safe conduct, King Thorstein?" Raud demanded, his voice carrying over the sound of the besieging army in the distance. "You have nothing to fear," Thorstein replied calmly. "As long as you come in peace." The two chiefs approached cautiously, their men watching from a safe distance. Thorstein's soldiers bristled with anticipation, but the King made no move to attack. He was a patient man, with a keen sense of strategy, and he knew that diplomacy was the key to victory. "I am Raud the Strong," the first chief announced, his voice booming. "And this is Thori Hart. We know who you are, Thorstein Triggveson. But the question is: have you come in peace or in war?" Thorstein laughed, a genuine sound that echoed across the rocky shore. "It's funny you should ask that, Raud, when you and your men have been attacking us for weeks. But to answer your question, I am here to talk." The two chiefs exchanged a heated glance, clearly not expecting this response. But they didn't back down. "You have caught us at a disadvantage," Raud said, his tone gruff. "But we will not surrender so easily.

We will fight you to the last." Thorstein shook his head, a small frown creasing his forehead. "I don't want to fight you, Raud. I want a peaceful resolution. I have your ships, I have more men than you, and I have the upper hand. But I'm not interested in bloodshed. If you agree to lay down your arms and abandon your revolt, you can go home unharmed." Thori Hart looked surprised. "But we thought you were forcing all your subjects to be baptized. Do we have to convert?" Thorstein smiled ruefully. "No, Thori. Baptism is a choice, not a punishment. All the chiefs in this district have been baptized, but willingly. And I assure you, I am not interested in forcing anyone to follow my religion. I only want what's best for my people." Raud and Thori conferred quietly for a moment, whispering in each other's ears. Finally, Raud stepped forward, his face set in a scowl. "We accept your terms, King Thorstein. But know this: we will not forget this humiliation. We will regroup, and we will come back stronger. And when we do, we will not be so easily defeated." Thorstein nodded, his eyes glinting with respect. "I wouldn't expect any less, Raud. But for now, let's end this conflict and seek peace. It's what Odin would want." And with that, the two chiefs turned and strode back to their camp, their men following close behind. Thorstein watched them go, a sense of relief flooding through him. He knew this was only the beginning of his fight to keep his people safe and united, but for now, the battle was won.

The conquering King Thorstein, wearily acknowledged the defeated warriors before him, noting their gratitude for their lives. Although their capitulation was appreciated, he couldn't help but feel a sense of incompleteness. Thorstein had mastered all that had stood against him, yet still felt incomplete in some way. As a vassal of Jesus Christ and servant of God, he knew his quest for spiritual enlightenment was far from over. Raud, one of the strongest priests of Thor in the north, caught his eye. Thorstein noticed the glint of defiance in Raud's gaze, even after everything he had been through. Raud knew the power of his heathen gods, and Thorstein knew his God. Not yet ready to coerce Raud into accepting his faith, Thorstein offered an ingenious proposition. They would each pray to their respective gods, and then wrestle. The victor, the one who first threw the other to the ground, would be the winner, and therefore obligated to bestow their faith on the opposing army's men. This proposal was accepted by both parties. Thorstein stepped confidently into the field of battle, trusting in his god to guide him. He knew that whatever the outcome of the match, he was in the hands of his Father in heaven. Raud, on the other hand, was almost giddy with excitement. He was extremely proficient in wrestling, and he knew he had a chance to prove his worth. Despite the bitter cold, the anticipation of the upcoming match, and the scent of danger thick in the air, the two armies stood united in their excitement. The space cleared out for the match shone brightly in the light of the great fire that had been built to keep them warm. On one side, the warriors of King Thorstein, frozen yet determined, and on the other, the followers of heathen Raud, smirking in their confidence of victory. The two men stepped into the arena, their armor discarded, and took hold of each other. The crowd was silent as they watched intently, suspending their breath in anticipation. The two men grappled at each other, each trying to out-muscle the other. Then they both fell, bodies wrestling on the snow-covered ground. In the end, Thorstein emerged victorious. He finally felt a sense of completion in his conquest of Raud, and was eager to spread the love of the Lord. In death, Raud would be saved by the sacrifice of a Holy God. As for the spectators, they simply rejoiced in the thrill of the match that had proven, once and for all, who was the strongest man in all the land.

Chapter 26

THE CROSS AND THE HAMMER

S igurd's heart sank as he observed the massive muscles and powerful limbs of the pagan fighter before him. However, he glanced at his ally Thorstein, and although his muscles were not as large, Sigurd knew that Thorstein possessed tremendous strength. At the start of the bout, the opponents tactfully evaluated each other. Gradually, Raud increased his intensity and made tremendous attempts to overthrow Thorstein. However, to the amazement of the crowd, Thorstein resisted every effort, appearing to do so without exerting any effort. The disparity between the two men's lifestyles became apparent. As Raud rapidly lost his breath, became flushed and exhausted, King Thorstein remained fresh and alert due to his temperate habits. As the Viking weakened, Thorstein unexpectedly took hold of Raud's thigh in an unguarded moment and with a swift motion, flung him over his head. His companions roared with delight, while Raud's men groaned in despair as their leader hit the ground. Thorstein rushed to his opponent's side. In an act of courtesy, Thorstein assisted the fallen man who was struggling to rise. "You beat me fairly, Thorstein," Raud exclaimed, looking at his adversary with wondering eyes. "I owe my life to you." "No," responded the benevolent King, offering the Viking his attire. "I do not seek anyone's blood, Raud. All I ask is for you to work for me faithfully, and you will receive the same land that you received from Ragnvald." Expeditiously,

messengers were dispatched to Nidaros to report the outcome of the confronta-
tion. Subsequently, after Raud, Thori, and his soldiers had willingly undergone
baptism. Thorstein and his troops boarded their ships and returned south. As
the Firth was closed again, the ships were pulled ashore for the winter, and
the bonders' leaders left the king for their abodes. Meanwhile, Thorstein and
his men climbed over the snow-covered hills. At Ladi, they crossed the ice to
Nidaros, receiving a warm greeting. During Easter, Bishop Sigurd solemnized
the marriage between King Thorstein and Gudrun, Ironbeard's daughter. Additionally, Sigurd Fairhair and Freyja tied the knot, a wedding that did not
surprise anyone since the relationship between the two was widely known at the
court and they would marry sooner or later.

This Easter was a bit late, falling toward the end of April, and the Firth had been navigable for some time. As the procession left the church and wound its way through the streets of Nidaros toward the great hall, an astounding sight caught everyone's attention. A magnificent ship was making its way into the harbor. Its prow was shaped like a dragon's head, while its stern resembled the coils and tail of a dragon. Both ends were plated in gold, shining brilliantly in the early morning sun. The ship's sail had a dragon's wingspan, and the edges of the oars served as the beast's limbs. The people were astonished, but the king smiled at Sigurd and said, "I had this vessel built in secret, and now, it is my wedding present to my faithful Haldor, Sigurd Fairhair. It is not fitting for one of my Haldors to be landless, so I also bestow upon him the earldom of the Agdirs, and command that he make his wedding journey there in this vessel!" Four years later, King Thorstein Triggveson, along with a few of his ships, was tricked by the treacherous Haldor Sigvald in the islands of Svold Sound, while the majority of his fleet was at sea. There, his enemies, including the King of Sweden and King Harald of Denmark who had turned against him, and the heathen people of Norway who chose to abandon the land rather than accept the Cross, had gathered. One by one, the King's ships were seized, though he fought back like Norway had never seen. There was even a moment when King Thorstein seemed like he might turn the tables on his opponents, despite the odds. Unfortunately, Haldor Eirik, son of Haldor Ragnvald, tore the dragon-shaped heads off Thorstein's ships and attacked under the sign of the Cross. As the final few members of King Thorstein's army fell to the enemy's forecastle, he tossed aside his shield and dove into the water. He was well-known as a proficient swimmer among the nations of the north, and he dove deep and swam underneath his enemies' ships, making it appear that he had drowned. Emerging from the circle of ships, the King swam swiftly to a fishing boat that lay near the islands and was hoisted aboard by Sigurd and his wife Freyja. Unfortunately, they got there too late to warn the King about the betrayal. That night, with his wounds tended to, King Thorstein sat in the back of the boat, which sailed swiftly south.

Sigurd implored Thorstein to join his fleet and head north to fight the invaders, but the King refused. He explained his reasoning. Haldor Eirik had brandished a Cross during their battle, and Thorstein believed that Haldor had vowed to renounce the old gods if he emerged victorious. So, Thorstein believed Norway had finally become a Christian country, and he thought that God may have been displeased with his reign. Thus, he did not wish to return and cause more trouble. Freyja asked if they could travel to England together, as Thorstein had many powerful allies there, including King Beornwulf. But once more, Thorstein refused. He wished to leave Norway and become a pilgrim. He planned to visit Rome and Jerusalem and join the Crusaders to fight against the Muslims. When Sigurd realized that he could not change Thorstein's mind, he gave up and returned to his earldom of Agdir. Thorstein stayed for a fortnight before deciding to leave, fearing that his presence could cause problems for friends. Thorstein offered Sigurd and his lands to the conquerors and selected a small ship with a score of men to leave Norway forever. As they raised the anchor, Thorstein, Sigurd, and Freyja stood together on the forecastle, and the King spoke a sad farewell.

"My dear friends, trust me when I say that this is for the better. Peace will finally descend upon our land. The faith of Christ has taken root, and though some may at times revert to the old ways of our ancestors, I believe it will only be a fleeting moment. Here, take hold of my sword, as you did once before in Ireland, and carry it as a memento of me. I shall never wield a weapon again, except to defend the sacred ground of the Holy Land." With tears streaming down their faces, Sigurd and Freyja hugged the King tightly, bidding him farewell as they disembarked from the ship. Within an hour, the vessel was a mere speck on the distant horizon. "Come, Freyja," spoke Sigurd, voice choked with emotion. "We may never lay eyes upon Thorstein again, but he will always be remembered as the first King of Norway to depose the Hammer of Thor and raise high the symbol of the Cross of Christ!".

THE END.

Bonus

Free Bonus

Download the book "Viking Fervor" free at **Shadowplay.com/Vikings**. Also, get the Audiobook version, also free.

Information on receiving FREE promotional copies of upcoming books and audiobooks

Shadowplay.com/Vikings

Printed in Great Britain
by Amazon

43626775R00086